Tales in Trees

MARY ROBERTSON

ISBN 978-1-954345-17-1 (paperback)
ISBN 978-1-954345-18-8 (digital)

Rushmore Press LLC
1 800 460 9188
www.rushmorepress.com

Printed in the United States of America

Prologue

Evelyn had just found out not too long ago that there was much more to her than she realized. Her life had been turned upside down when she found out that she belonged to a long-forgotten Indian tribe as their long-awaited Pale Granddaughter. She was about to graduate and be reunited with the soon-to-be chief, Anthony. The wait from December was so hard, but now, time was closing in on their reunion.

Chapter 1

Evelyn looked into the mirror and smiled. Grandma helped her fix her hair. It was braided back on one side, and she carefully put her owl feather at the bottom.

"Thank you, Grandma," Evey said, turning to hug the short, round woman with a grey bun fixed atop her head.

Sometimes Every thought it strange that just six short months ago, she had no clue she had an entire family outside her grandma, grandpa, and herself. As she looked in the mirror, she could see the best of both worlds—pale face and Indian. She smiled as she touched the feather tied in at the bottom of her braid. It was a gift from the owls on one of the last nights she spent with Anthony.

Oh, Anthony, she thought as a smile came to her lips, thinking about her muscular tall, tan Indian who could go from a man with the most heartwarming smile to a warrior by her side in an instant.

She missed him terribly. They had only been intimate the one time, and she longed for his touch.

Grandma studied her granddaughter.

"I can tell you're thinking of Anthony. Your whole face smiles when you do," she said, patting Evey's hand.

Evelyn smiled at her and said, "I am. I can't wait to see him next week."

Grandma returned the smile and said, "That's great and all, but now we have to get you to the school so you can graduate. We are so proud of you, honey."

"That we are, sister! You make us all look smart," her blue-eyed, handsome short Grandpa spoke from her doorway. "You look real pretty."

Grandma nodded in agreement and said, "It's time for us to go."

Evelyn rode in between her grandparents as usual in the old, light blue single-cab Chevy truck. There was always so much security sitting in the middle of them. She loved them so much. She was nervous about leaving next week and being away from them.

Evey was going to go back to New Mexico to reunite with Anthony and her people. She never really had spent much time away from them since her parents died, but they assured her they would be fine and so would she. It was important for her to find her own life and be with the one who sets her soul on fire, and there was no doubt that was Anthony. From the first moment she saw him, they were connected. There was no real explanation, but they were destined for one another.

They pulled into the driveway at the small town school. Evey cringed when she saw her ex, Danny, pull in at the same time.

"You okay, sister? Do you want me to walk you in?" her grandpa asked, staring dubiously at the newer Chevy truck that had just pulled in.

She hadn't spoken to Danny since finding out he had been trying to marry her to get a hold of her family land. He swore that he had real feelings for her and even went as far as asking her to marry him at the Indian reservation. She had turned him down when she had held the Bailey ring in her palm and seen what he and his awful mother had been planning. Unfortunately with her visions, she could produce no actual proof of the terrible things they did. It was just her word. The fact was, however, that her feelings for him had been real and he had hurt her more badly than she thought possible. But she dodged a bullet and was glad because the door that had been shut opened a much happier one.

"I'll be okay, Grandpa. Thank you," she said, and he nodded.

Grandma opened the door and stepped off the truck to let Evey out.

Evelyn started walking toward the football field. They hosted graduation out here because nowhere else in their tiny school could hold enough people. She locked eyes with Danny and stood up taller. She would not show weakness around him. She clutched at her necklaces around her neck—one was Sarah's, a leather necklace with an old stone in the middle that had belonged to the first chief of their tribe and the other was also a handmade leather necklace, made by Anthony, with the snake rattler her grandpa had given her. The rattler was supposed to be good luck, and she sure hoped so. She would have to see some people she really didn't want to after learning so much about them, Danny being one and his mother being the other.

Danny was waiting for her to approach, but Evey had every intention of just walking past him.

When he reached his hand out delicately and just said, "Evey," it was almost too quiet to hear.

She looked up to meet his eyes. His sad blue eyes, she noticed. She didn't say anything and just looked at him.

He went on barely louder than a whisper, as if it hurt him to talk, "Evey, I'm so sorry. I truly am. I hope you believe me. It really was all my mother's plan, but I was young and didn't know any better and went along with it, and I was wrong. Please believe me. I do love you, and I always will. I understand your need to hate me, and I don't blame you, but please don't think you meant nothing to me. You mean everything to me, and I didn't know how to do the right thing, and I'm sorry."

Danny searched her face for her emotions, but she stood blank for a moment and then took a breath.

"I don't hate you, Danny. I choose not to hate anyone who would only hurt me more," Evey said. "I'm sorry for what happened between us too. I should have been smart enough to see through it all, and I wasn't. I will forgive you in time because doing so will set me free too. But I'm not ready yet. We need to go and get in our places."

She took his hand off her arm and then walked past him to find her seat.

Danny stood a little while longer looking at the ground, and Evey could have sworn he was fighting back tears.

Chapter 2

The graduation started. They started with a prayer, followed by the singing of the national anthem, the salutatorian speech, and then they announced the valedictorian.

"Now for the valedictorian of this senior class, Evelyn Ermis."

The crowd applauded, and Evey took a deep breath and stood up to make her way to the podium. She got up there and smiled. She had learned from one of her teachers that smiling while speaking helped.

"First, I would like to thank everyone here in attendance for coming to see us take the next step in our lives," Evey started her speech. "Crossing this stage is the closing of one chapter and the start of another. Sitting among us may be doctors, lawyers, teachers, American heroes, but today we are just us. Tomorrow we will start the journey of adult life and seeking to find what our passions truly are. Some of us may have that figured out, but I think what sets one apart is being able to recognize that life is messy, and sometimes you have to just go with it and put the pieces together as you go.

"It's okay to not have everything figured out and to learn from our past and present. For me, having the love and support of my family has given me a strength that I didn't know was in me, and I'll forever be grateful for the unconditional love and advice. As valedictorian, I know how to work hard, study, write papers, and ace exams, and I'm supposed to depart my class with some sort of advice. The truth is, I don't really have any. I'm in the same boat as all of you.

"A smart woman told me to find what sets my soul on fire, whether that be a person or a job. May we all be blessed enough to find both. Let's go out and make something great out of this place. Seniors rule!"

The class erupted into whoops and yelps of joy. She looked over to see the happy faces and jubilation, and she smiled in return. She had been in school with most of the forty-three students since kindergarten. She met Danny's eyes on accident, and he just nodded at her. She smiled.

She went back to her seat, and the graduation commenced. All forty-three students had their names read, along with their list of achievements. Then it was time to play their class song in the middle of the field, and they all huddled together in a small circle. Their class song was "Free Bird." It wasn't Evey's number one choice, but it was a democracy and the girls got outvoted. She smiled, looking at the faces around her.

When the song ended, they all hooped and hollered and threw a huge beach ball around and, finally, threw their caps in the air. It was finished. She was done and had done well.

Everyone's friends and family made their way onto the field to find their graduate to give them cards and take pictures. Evelyn's blood ran cold when she saw Danny's mom, Mrs. Bailey.

Mrs. Bailey knew everything. She knew her ancestor had murdered her family, and she had put a plan in motion to try to get Evey to marry her son so they could acquire Evey's family land. She disliked this woman so much. She was arrogant and treated everyone like they were beneath her. Evey got to experience that firsthand at one of her dinner parties.

Evey stiffened and stood taller. She looked Mrs. Bailey in her cold gray eyes. Mrs. Bailey just smiled at her. Evey felt sick. Mrs. Bailey was walking toward her, and luckily, her grandparents made it to her side in time.

"Evey we are so proud of you! Your speech was short, sweet, and on point. We love you," Grandma said as she and Grandpa both swooped in to hug Evey.

Grandma eyed Mrs. Bailey dispassionately.

"Well, hi there, Mrs. Bailey. Our Evey was just great, wasn't she? Our smart girl," Grandma said with extra sugar on top.

"Yes. Very smart," Mrs. Bailey said, nodded, and kept walking.

Danny was walking toward his mother and Evey when he all the sudden stood stark still.

Chapter 3

"I am proud to be in this moment with you," said a boy in an Indian language that only few knew.

Evey whirled around shocked to see Anthony. She jumped into his arms, and he grabbed her tight and spun her around. She hadn't even seen him sneak up behind her with all the excitement. He kissed her.

"How did you . . . when did you . . ." Evey trailed off, seeing the other two women with him.

"Belle, Analac!" she screamed as Anthony set her down, lunging at the women to hug their necks as tight as she could.

Evey had felt like a piece of her was missing since leaving the reservation, and now the pieces were back with her. They were all smiling so big that their cheeks hurt.

Anthony was behind Evey with his arms around her, laughing with everyone, as they told her they decided they would surprise her on her graduation. Her grandparents were in on it too.

"I can't believe you all did this for me! This is the best graduation gift ever. I've missed you all so much, and to have you here, my family . . ." Evey trailed off, moisture filling her eyes.

"No, we aren't going to cry. We are proud that our Pale Granddaughter kicked butt," Analac said with her big toothless smile.

Danny felt sick. He was going to go congratulate Evey when he saw the big Indian quietly come up behind her. Anthony had locked eyes with Danny and gave him a stare that would keep anyone at bay.

She was so happy to see him. Any fool could see that. Mrs. Bailey followed her son's gaze to see what or who he was looking at.

She scoffed and said, "Well, look at that. Looks like we are being invaded. People should just stick with their own."

"Mom, she thinks they are her people. She even speaks their language, and they didn't try to trick her," Danny said, feeling a tinge of anger toward his mother.

"Well, I guess I should go tell them hi," Mrs. Bailey said, smirking.

"Mother, no," was all Danny managed before she was making her way through the crowd to Evey's happy reunion.

"Evelyn, darling, I wanted to come tell you congratulations. I know you've worked hard to get to this point. Oh my, and who are your lovely friends?" Mrs. Bailey asked with such a fake smile that Evey wanted to slap it off her face.

Evey tightened in Anthony's arms, and he squeezed her in reassurance.

"Thank you, Mrs. Bailey. It really wasn't necessary for you to walk all the way over to tell me," Evey said.

"Oh, but it was, and who are these people?" she asked, waving her hand toward Belle and Analac.

"These wonderful ladies are my family, and this is Anthony," she said, patting his hand. "The beat of my heart."

Mrs. Bailey looked taken aback.

"Oh well, yes. Nice to meet you all. I'm Danny's mother, and we own all the property along the county line," she said.

"Oh, indeed," Belle added, smiling. "We know who you are, Mrs. Bailey, and we take care of our own too. Just like you."

Mrs. Bailey's eyes went wide at that proclamation.

Evey smiled, and Grandma and Grandpa were thoroughly pleased with Belle's reaction. They were trying not to laugh.

Mrs. Bailey nodded at that and turned on her heel and walked back to Danny. Danny gave the group a look that seemed like he was sorry.

"It seems like Danny feels bad," Grandma said, looking at the boy.

"He does. He told me as much earlier. Mrs. Bailey is just such a nasty woman. I almost feel sorry for him," Evey said, and Anthony held her tighter.

Anthony didn't even like her mentioning Danny, much less know that she talked to him. All the ladies sighed and nodded, but Grandpa and Anthony had different opinions on Danny.

"I have the right mind to beat him in front of his mother now that I know his cousin wouldn't be there to jump on my back," Anthony said, giving his best warrior stare in that direction.

Grandpa nodded in agreement. "That boy could use a good whooping."

"Grandpa, Anthony! Seriously, we've won. That would do us no good at this point," Evey said.

"I seem to remember you having swollen knuckles after beating his face in pretty well, Evey," said Anthony, looking at her with a crooked grin.

"Well then, that's enough, isn't it?" she asked, smiling.

"If you say so," he said.

"Oh what I would have given to see you pounding on him," Grandpa laughed.

"I think it's time we head home," Grandma broke in. "I have a dinner to cook."

Everyone was happy at that announcement, and the two older Indian ladies were excited to go back to the farm and help.

They made it back to the farmhouse, and everyone was getting out when Analac exclaimed, "Pale Granddaughter, I hear your tree."

"You hear my tree, Analac?" Evey asked.

"Yes, Daughter. My gift," she smiled at Evey and was making her way toward the tree that Evey had used as her special place all her life and where they had found some of the missing pieces of a long-lost couple.

Evey looked at Anthony. She hoped the tree wouldn't tell her everything. Anthony must have realized what Evey was thinking because a huge smile broke out on his handsome face. It didn't seem to bother him. She grabbed his hand, and they followed Analac. Analac made it through the gate and walked over to the tree humming. Anthony and Evey were behind and made sure to close the gate.

"Oh yes," said Analac as she moved to the tree and rested her hands on it.

She smiled, cried, and then smiled again. She looked up at Anthony and Evelyn.

"This tree has seen and been through a lot." Her eyes seemed to say they knew more than her lips were saying.

Anthony cleared his throat.

"Yes, it has seen a lot. We told you about Apovini and Pale Daughter burying their special possessions here."

"Oh yes, you told me, but the tree has seen more than that. It has been a friend to many ladies in Pale Daughter's family. It holds your secrets, dreams, and fears. And it holds love," Analac said, smiling at them.

She walked away from the tree humming and came to the young couple and put a hand on each of their faces and smiled.

"Your souls are on fire. Take care of each other. You will be like this tree and weather many storms together but be made strong."

Evey let go of Anthony's hand and hugged Analac tight enough to send the air from her lungs.

"Ooof! Daughter, I love you like you're my own," Analac said, squeezing Evey back just as tight.

"I am your own," Evey said.

Anthony was smiling at such a warm exchange and had to hold a laugh in when Analac looked up at him and nodded back at the tree and wiggled her eyebrows. Oh yes, she knew.

Tudley came bounding in from the field.

"And who is this?" Analac laughed as the pet coyote, whom Evey had raised, licked her leg.

"This is Tudley, my baby," said Evey.

"And here I thought your baby was Anthony," Analac chuckled as she bent down to scratch the furry fellow between the ears.

Anthony made a face at her. Tudley was happy, and then he ran over to Anthony, happy to see him.

"I missed you too," Anthony said, wiping the slobber from his face where Tudley licked him.

Tudley followed them as they went.

The three of them walked back to the farmhouse. Belle was smiling. The wind always brought her news on it. She had heard the exchange on the whispers of the wind. They would be strong together. They all made their way inside.

Grandma made a Texas sheet cake, and Evey could hardly wait to get into it. The ladies worked on supper together. Analac snapped green beans, Belle worked on garlic bread, and Grandma made spaghetti. That was easy to do in a hurry and feeds a lot. They all squeezed in around the table. It was a tight fit, but no one complained. They were family and seeing the table full sent such a happiness through them all.

They discussed their plans for the rest of the week and talked about Anthony's upcoming ceremony to be named chief of their people, and they discussed the Baileys. They wished they could get them in some sort of legal trouble, but they couldn't.

"I think them knowing that we truly know the whole truth will put a stop to them," Grandma said. "Now that we know, there is no way we will even let them look at this land. Oh, Belle, I love what you said to Mrs. Bailey! You could literally see the blood drain from her face."

"I meant it," Belle laughed. "We take care of each other. I hope she doesn't try to pull anything else, but if she does, we will handle it together."

Grandpa looked at Anthony and asked, "How did we get so lucky to be the only two men with all these smart, beautiful ladies?"

All the women gushed, and Grandpa said, "Lesson number one—know when they are smarter than you and you are outnumbered. And always give compliments. A good compliment has gotten me out of trouble plenty of times."

Everyone laughed, and Grandma whooped Grandpa's arm with a tea towel.

After eating and changing into blue jeans and a T-shirt, Evey told Anthony to come walk with her to check cows and check the windmill. None of them really needed checking, but she just wanted to steal away with him for a moment.

"As I was walking to check a calf last winter, this is where I stumbled across the rattlesnake whose rattler is now around my neck," she was telling Anthony as he swooped her up off her feet into a big, warm hug.

It was May, and it was hot out, even in the evening. They were sweating, but it didn't matter. He just needed to touch her. He had her held up over his face, and she leaned down the few inches and kissed his mouth.

When she picked her head back up, she said, "I've missed you so much. My heart feels whole again. I don't want to ever be parted from you again."

He picked his mouth up to meet hers once more and then said, "You don't ever have to be. You are my everything now."

He sat her down, and Tudley barked, thinking they were playing a game. She linked her fingers in with his, and they walked toward the windmill. Tudley ran off, more interested in cow patties. She told him how the windmill that pumped water into the cow trough worked and how she and Grandpa had to fix it every now and then, and he listened with true sincerity and wondered how he got so lucky to be able to call Evey his. She could do anything. He loved how her face lit up when she talked about fixing things and caring for the animals.

Evey stopped midsentence to see him just staring at her with a smile on his face, and she said, "What?"

He took her face in his hands and said, "I love you. I love everything about you. How you light up telling me all the things you've done and how the sweat is just stuck right at you hairline by your ears and how the sun makes your eyes look like they are on fire. God, Evey, I love you."

She melted into him and whispered, "You are the beat of my heart, and without you I'm dead on the inside. I love you."

And they kissed with a passion most people dream of having.

At that time, a brown-and-white heifer came walking over and put her wet nose right in the middle of the two in love people.

Evey started laughing.

"Doe, are you jealous?"

Doe was a little calf that Evey had helped care for the previous winter, and it was quite attached to her.

"Doe, is it?" Anthony asked.

"Yes, this is Doe. She is one of my babies," she said, still laughing at the rude interruption.

"Did you name her that because of her eyes?" Anthony wondered out loud.

Evey looked up surprised at him and said, "Yes. Yes I did. You really are linked to me, aren't you?"

He just smiled at her. She pushed Doe off and made her way to the cattle pin across the way. She climbed through the fence to a little closed-off feed room. Anthony followed her. She opened a bin and a sweet molasses smell filled the air.

She looked at him, smiling. "Sweet feed. Doe loves it. It'll keep her busy for a bit."

She took a small bucket and scooped some up and went and poured it on the other side of the fence. Anthony just watched her. She was muscular but not too muscular, still very feminine. Her jeans were tight on her butt and thighs, and he was getting a burning sensation and he tried to look away. Before he couldn't hide his thoughts, she caught his eyes and smiled wide. She nodded her head toward the little feed room, and he followed.

It was tiny, and there was hay everywhere and two bins filled with feed and another bin filled with milk replacer. There were halters and ropes hung on nails on the wall and a little shelf with the huge milk bottles they would sometimes have to use for calves. He also noticed a blanket in the corner and raised his eyebrows in inquiry.

"Sometimes we have to pull calves when the weather is bad or the new baby will get really sick. I will bring them in here and sometimes spend all night with them nursing them back to health. Sometimes the best thing for them is to just be held and rubbed. I've never brought anyone in here—well, except Grandpa. He would bring me breakfast and help me when I needed it. He built this little feed room just to hold feed, but we had to pull a calf one winter, and it was so rainy and the wind would cut right through you, and the wind was blowing rain in this pin.

"There was nowhere to put the calf, so I opened the feed room, and Grandpa brought it in, and I cared for it all night. Its mother died, and she was my responsibility then. Having a responsibility helped me keep going, after my parents died. Anyway, Doe belongs to the calf I nursed all night, and this is my little room to care for them, when need be. Watch your head. It's not high enough to stand in," she explained to him as she set the blanket out.

It was clear she had the same thing on her mind as he did. She knelt as she couldn't stand straight up and started taking off her shirt.

"Wait. Let me do it," Anthony told her.

She smiled and stopped and waited for him to get to her. In two awkward, bent steps, he closed the gap in between them and bent down to his knees to be on her level. He wrapped her up in his arms and kissed her and pulled back to look in her eyes. The hunger in hers mirrored his.

"I love you," he said, taking her shirt the rest of the way off and unclasping her bra.

She pulled her arms out of the straps and smiled at him. He smiled back, looking at her perfect round breasts. She slid her hands up his shirt to feel his hard, muscular chest and realized she had missed him more than she thought. She pulled him to her and kissed him urgently. She ripped his shirt up, and then she moaned as their bare chests collided. They had hair and hands flying everywhere. They were both already slippery from sweat, and they glided on each other easily.

He unbuttoned her fly, she giggled, and in turn, he laughed. She unbuttoned his too and in one motion slid them down past his hips to find out he had been commando all this time. She couldn't help but smile at this. He ripped her pants down and lay her back gently on the blanket she had set out, with his arm securely behind her to guide the way. He lay beside her, kissing her and touching her the way she had longed to be touched all these long months. His hands were like magic, and she arched her back and gasped for air. She reached down and found him erect and tall for her. She gently stroked him to return the favor.

He grabbed her hand to stop her and said, "Slowly. Let me love you right."

She about lost her senses. He was so perfect to her—her Indian, her beat of her heart.

When he thought she couldn't handle it anymore, he made his way on top of her and so very slowly put himself inside her and moved slowly. He wanted it to last. It would be hard to since it had been so many months since their first and only intimate encounter under her oak tree. He loved her, and he wanted her to feel it in her body as well.

She wrapped her legs around him to pull him in deeper to her, and he moaned. She had her hands in his hair and pulled him down to her to kiss him with passion. He loved her deeply, and she wanted more.

"Anthony," she said.

He looked at her in question as he moved slowly.

"Anthony, have your way," she pleaded.

He looked down at her and shook his head and plowed into her deeply, and she shrieked with excitement. He liked her little sounds, and those sounds urged him harder and faster until they were both on the edge of oblivion.

He rolled off her, panting and sweating. She looked at him and laughed.

"What are you laughing at?" he said.

She pointed to his head. He felt it and felt little pieces of hay sticking out, and then he laughed, taking a closer inspection of her. She had hay all in her hair too and could have passed for a scarecrow.

"We might need to get the hay out of hair before we walk back," Evey said.

"How about we get dressed first, and then I'll help you work on that head," Anthony said, smiling at her. "Damn, I missed you, Evey."

He firmly grasped one of her breasts. She laughed and slapped his hand and started to find all the pieces of her clothes.

Chapter 5

They made their way back to the house, still picking hay off each other, talking and laughing. It was so easy for them to just be together. They loved just spending time with each other. Although the intimacy was great, they just truly enjoyed being friends.

When they made it back up to the farmhouse, Analac was outside walking around the trees and looking at the chickens, with Tudley following her.

"What are you doing, Analac?" asked Evey.

"I'm just listening to the trees and enjoying this place. I love chickens, and the company isn't too bad," Analac said, smiling her toothless smile and nodding toward Tudley.

Evey and Anthony walked over to her.

"And what are you two doing?" Analac asked as she picked a piece of hay out of Evey's hair, eyeing them with a goofy grin.

"I think the tree already told you, didn't it?" Anthony asked, and Evey was just about ready to die.

"Ha-ha! Well, sometimes I find out a little more than I need to, but hey, you're young and in love. Enjoy it. My lips are sealed. Oh to be your age again," Analac said with a dreamy smile.

"I love you Analac," Evey said, laughing.

"And I love you, and I expect to have a front-row seat to your marriage day," Analac said.

"Done," said Anthony, looking at Evey smiling.

"Oh come here, Pale Granddaughter," Analac said and began to pick the hay out that Anthony missed.

"Anthony, did you get any out?" Evey asked him, looking at him.

"I did. It was just a lot," he said sheepishly.

Analac was chuckling.

It was getting late. The sun stayed out longer, so it was almost nine when it got dark. Evey made her way in and went straight to the bathroom to shower and didn't stop to talk to anyone in case there were more hay stuck in her hair. She got in there and stripped and looked in the mirror and smiled at herself. She was so happy. She noticed a little strawberry on her ribs under her left breast and wondered when that happened and just laughed. She didn't mind being marked by her love.

She checked her hair, and it looked like Analac got most of the hay out. She laughed quietly to herself. She had envisioned her and Anthony's reunion over and over in her mind. She had no idea he was coming to her graduation and the impromptu roll in the hay was just that—unplanned. But she had to have him. It was like the whole ground shook when they were joined. She took off her necklaces and took the feather out of her hair and showered.

Evey was blissfully tired when she got out. Anthony was waiting for his turn and must have heard her turn the water off because he was in the hall, waiting when she came out, and he snuck a kiss from her on his way in. She made her way to the kitchen to see the old folks having a piece of Texas sheet cake and drinking coffee.

She sat down to join them. The chocolatey cake melted away in her mouth, and she opted for milk so close to bed time. She just sat and listened to them visiting and smiled and enjoyed being surrounded by the people whom she trusted and loved.

"Evey, how about you come home with us when we leave on Tuesday?" Belle asked.

"Oh I'd love too, but Grandpa needs me to help him here," Evey said.

"Don't worry. Anthony can be an extra set of hands to help you get whatever needs to be done, and it will be nice to have you there to help prepare for Anthony ceremony," Belle explained.

Evey looked at her grandparents.

They smiled.

"It's okay, sister. You go. We will get everything done, and your grandma and I will be coming up for the ceremony to see Anthony become chief."

Evey's eyes brightened. She was so happy they would make it and that she could go home early with Anthony.

Anthony made his way to the kitchen after his shower with nothing but cotton shorts on. Everyone looked at him, smiling. He smiled back and walked over to the table to steal a bite of Evey's cake.

"Hey, get your own!" she shrieked as he made a smacking sound on her fork.

He laughed, mouth full of cake, and said, "I thought what yours was mine and mine was yours now?"

She giggled, and everyone at the table watched the exchange, smiling. Their love for each other just flowed from them.

At bedtime, it was cramped. The tiny farmhouse was used to only three. Evey gave her room to Belle and Analac. She had a queen-sized bed, and the two women could share. Anthony would sleep on the couch, and it seemed as if Tudley would sleep by him. He loved Anthony. Evey would take the small loft bed in the small upstairs room. It had been a long time since she slept up there. Everyone went to bed and were asleep fast. It had been a long day.

But Evey was still awake and she smiled when she heard the narrow wooden stairs creak under the weight of someone slowly coming up. Anthony smiled at the top of the stair as soon as she could see him. She smiled back and scooted over. It was a twin-sized bed, and the two of them fitting in there would mean they would essentially have to be connected at the hip.

He slid in behind her and pulled her in close to him and just held her. Their breathing slowed together, and she fell fast asleep in the comfort of his arms and his breathing on the back of her neck.

Chapter 6

Evey woke up startled to light coming in the single window. She realized that Anthony was no longer in her bed. She wondered if he made it out in time before anyone woke to find they had slept together, but they had really only slept. She thought of how she could sleep in his arms. She didn't dream crazy dreams—she just slept.

She stretched her arms toward the ceiling and grunted. She got out of the small bed, made the bed, and decided she and Anthony would have to get a king-sized bed eventually. Grandma was a stickler on a made bed. She smiled again, thinking about Anthony holding her.

"What are you smiling about?" Evey heard Anthony say from the doorway.

"You," she replied, smiling right at him now. "When did you leave?"

"I think it was about three this morning. I woke up panicked, thinking it was too late already, but it all ended up being fine," he said, winking at her.

She finished placing the pillows and met him at the doorway and walked down the steps. Like a gentleman, he let her go first or it could have been he just wanted to watch her bottom as she went down.

Grandpa was making breakfast. It was Sunday, and Sunday was always his day to make breakfast. It was always pancakes, bacon, eggs, and coffee. Grandma's morning off, he would say. Evey walked over to the stove and kissed his cheek and told him good morning.

He smiled at her, and she poured her a cup of coffee, and then it hit her. It was Sunday—church day!

"Are we going to church this morning?" she asked Grandpa.

"Well of course. We go every Sunday, and Belle and Analac said they would come too," he told her.

Evey felt nervous. Their small town was weary of newcomers, and they would be bringing Indians—her people. But in the same instant she didn't care; they would become her family too.

"I'd like to see what this preacher has to say," said Analac, rounding the corner to the table already dressed in a beautiful Aztec print dress and red beaded earrings.

"You look lovely, Analac," said Evey.

Analac smiled and told her thank you in their language.

"Plus, I hear the Baileys go to church there too, and I wouldn't want to miss a chance to see a good look of surprise on Mrs. Bailey's face," continued Analac, looking mischievous.

"Oh, I second that," said Grandma, walking in and stealing a kiss from Grandpa.

Anthony was laughing out loud now. He couldn't help it. He felt bad for anyone who crossed all these women. Grandpa seemed to share Anthony's thoughts exactly.

"Anthony, I think we should each sit on an end in the pew at church and keep these cackling hens in between us," Grandpa said to Anthony.

"Yes, sir. I think that would be smart. My grandmother is liable to jump over a pew to defend Evey," he said, laughing.

"And is that so wrong?" Belle said laughing, walking into the kitchen in a beautiful blue Sunday dress with her beaded necklace.

"No it isn't. I'd do the same," said Grandma.

Evey felt so loved and a little nervous, but it would be fun to see everyone's faces when she and her people came waltzing in.

Evey ate breakfast quickly and then ran to her room to get dressed. She wasn't sure what to wear. She sat on her bed and looked in her closet for a minute.

If we are going to stick out, might as well do it in fashion, Evey thought as she got up and made her way to her closet.

She pulled out a bright yellow dress, with a yellow satin underlay and yellow lace on top. It was form fitting but covered her up. It had three-quarter sleeves and went down to her knees, but it hugged all the right places. She picked out a white pair of short heels. She looked in the mirror at her hair. It was wild and all over the place. She brushed to find she just looked like a lion with an extra fluffy mane. She laughed and looked over to the door to see Belle watching her with a smile on her face.

"Hey, Belle," Evey said.

"Granddaughter of my heart, you are beautiful, wild hair and all," she told her, walking toward her. "Can I help you with your hair?"

"Of course, I never turn down help with my hair," Evey said, smiling at her.

"I never had any daughters, until my son married Anthony's mother. I was so happy. She was a sweet spirit but loved my son more than life itself. When we lost him, she lost herself, and I lost my daughter. I'm blessed to have you, Evey," Belle told her, running her fingers through her hair.

Evey turned and hugged her. "And I'm blessed to have you. My family has always been so small, and having all of you makes me feel strong. I love you."

"And I love you. Let me fix your hair. How about a fishtail braid?" Belle asked.

"That sounds great," Evey said, turning to let Belle fix her hair.

Neither one of them heard Anthony step up in the hallway outside the door. He heard the two women he loved most love each other, and his heart bounded in his chest.

No, I'm the blessed one, he thought.

They made their way to church in two vehicles. Evey rode with her grandparents, and Belle followed them in her red Chevy Malibu. They pulled in and got out together. They would go in together and be a family. Grandma and Grandpa led the way, holding hands, and Belle and Analac linked together. Following up the rear was Anthony and Evey, holding hands.

"You ready to turn some heads?" she whispered to him.

"Always with you," he said, squeezing her hand for reassurance.

Boy, did heads turn.

Grandma and Grandpa greeted everyone kindly and introduced their guests. The congregation just stared at Anthony and Evey suspiciously. They didn't know the whole story of Danny and Evey's breakup, but now they assumed they knew why. Evey never uttered a word to anyone of what actually happened. It wouldn't matter.

Mrs. Bailey's jaw all but hit the floor when she saw all them walk in. Anthony was a huge presence. He was so tall and fierce, with sharp eyes. Everyone stared at him. Although he was in khakis, a white button-down shirt, and blue tie. It was obvious he was an Indian with his hair slicked back into a braid at the nape of his neck. Mrs. Bailey took their presence as a slap to the face. How dare Evey embarrass her family by showing up with her new Indian boyfriend, she thought.

Danny locked eyes with Anthony and nodded in a polite gesture to him. Anthony returned the nod, and Mrs. Bailey was ready to come unglued.

"Danny, seriously? Acknowledging that?" she whispered in disgust.

"Yes, Mother, acknowledging that. He loves her, and it does me no good to deny that. I've lost the only chance I had to be with someone so good, beautiful, and full of life," Danny snapped back.

"We will see about that," she said angrily.

Danny didn't say another word but wished his mother would drop it. Evey could have ruined their reputation if she would have spread the news of what she now knew, but she hadn't. Truth was, Evey was too good for all of them. Mrs. Bailey wasn't worried about it. She thought her family name would mean more than what one young girl could say.

Everyone found their seats. Grandpa sat on the end by the aisle, followed by Grandma, Belle, Analac, Evey, and Anthony. This was the first time Evey wasn't next to her grandma, but it was okay. She was next to the man whom she loved and Analac. Grandma was okay with that too. She felt safe knowing that so many loved her granddaughter as she did.

The preacher looked a little shocked when he saw their pew. The visitors were all so obviously Indian, and the boy was fierce and he showed no shame at all while holding Evelyn's hand on his leg. Evelyn made eye contact with him and smiled. He gave a weak smile back.

My goodness the girl is as bright as the sun in that yellow dress, the preacher thought. *Is she here to make a statement? But to who? Danny?*

Star-crossed young lovers were always a difficult situation in church. He would preach on forgiveness and love then. They made that decision for him.

Chapter 7

During the sermon, Evey looked at the ladies sitting next to her. She even saw Analac nod a few times in agreement with the preacher. It made her smile. When he preached on love, Anthony let go of her hand to wrap his arm around her shoulder. Talk about making people gasp—he was showing outward affection to her in church.

Analac grabbed Evey's hand and patted it. Finally at the end, they prayed, and the preacher dismissed them. Everyone's eyes were on the weird family leaving. On the way out, the preacher shook everyone's hand and told her grandparents it was so wonderful that they brought visitors with them.

"It was our pleasure to have our family here with us," Grandpa said, smiling, which made the preacher look dumbfounded.

Grandma squeezed Grandpa's arm, happy with his response to the preacher. Belle shook his hand and thanked him for a moving sermon and smiled at him, and to his astonishment, he smiled back at the pretty Indian women.

"Even preachers have eyes," Analac chuckled under her breath to Evey.

Evey laughed quietly too.

The preacher shook Analac's hand, and she told him, "I've lived almost ninety-five years on this earth, and I never get tired of hearing about love or forgiveness. Both are worthy to be preached on."

The preacher nodded at this and said, "Yes indeed. I'm glad you enjoyed it."

Then he got to Evey and Anthony. Anthony stepped forward as a man does, with Evey on his arm, and reached his hand out. The preacher took it, and Anthony shook his hand with a very firm grip.

"I've never had the pleasure of meeting you, young man," the preacher said, rubbing his hand after the strong handshake.

"I'm Anthony, sir," he said to the preacher.

"Nice to meet you, son. I hope some of my words got to you," the preacher said.

"Oh yes they did. It just confirms my love for this beautiful woman is true, and I will marry her at the first chance so our union can be made in the eyes of God," Anthony said, smiling and looking down into the preacher's eyes.

Evey had to hide a chuckle.

"Evey, it's so good to see you like normal, sweetie," the preacher said to her.

"And you as well, Preacher. Thank you for the word. It was very well spoken," Evey said, and they walked off.

Evelyn felt eyes watching her as she walked off with Anthony's strong arm around her. It could have been a number of astonished parishioners, but it so happened it was Mrs. Bailey watching them walk off, with contempt in her eyes.

Danny walked out, and the preacher shook his hand and said, "Heartbreaks can be hard son. I hope you find solace in the Lord and choose to forgive her."

"It's not her who needs to be forgiven. It's me," Danny said, to the preacher's bewilderment.

"Well, son, I'm here if you need to talk about it," the preacher told him.

"Thank you, sir," Danny replied.

He was doing his best to deal with his guilt and move on, but seeing Evey with another and in that dress—he just yearned for her. But Danny knew he couldn't have her. He knew he had messed up.

His mother looked at him with a pang of annoyance.

"Would you stop acting like you're the guilty party in all this? She left you," Mrs. Bailey said.

"I am the guilty party, and so are you," he said through clenched teeth.

She slapped him hard across the face.

"The only thing I'm guilty of is putting our family first and making sure you have the best of everything," she said, rubbing her hand on her leg.

Danny turned his head back and looked at her, furious.

"You will never lay a hand on me again. I will never have the best of everything because there she goes with someone else," he said and walked off away from her.

"Let him go," said Mr. Bailey, coming up beside his wife. "You two have caused a big enough scene out here. Thank God Evelyn is of more interest than a mother-and-son quarrel or you'd have more to answer for."

"Oh, darling. It is nothing. All will be fine soon," Mrs. Bailey said, eyes narrowed.

"Did you see Danny and his mother arguing?" Grandma asked Evey and Grandpa as they pulled out of the church parking lot.

"Yes I did," Grandpa said.

"He feels really bad about everything, and I don't think his mother feels the same way," Evey said.

"I'm sure not. She thinks that she is justified in whatever she does," Grandma said.

"I almost feel bad for Danny. To have a mother like that and lose a girl like you," Grandpa said. "But I don't."

Evey and Grandma laughed. Evey did in fact worry a little about him. If he really did feel bad and his mother knew, life would be hard for him.

They made their way back home and passed a little back road, and Evey looked to the side at it as they went by. She saw Danny's truck turning to go that way. It made her stomach tie up in a knot. That was the road they would sneak away for some time alone. You truly never lose a little of the love you have for your first, she thought. She almost smiled, thinking about it, and then turned to stone as she thought about him going along with his mother's wicked plan to acquire their land.

She still didn't know how he could do that to her. But then her features softened as she looked to the red car behind them. Anthony was driving, and he was laughing at something one of the older Indian ladies had said. She smiled. He was her life now, and she knew without a doubt she was his.

Chapter 8

They all made it back to the farmhouse, and Grandma and Belle worked together to heat up leftovers and make a couple new sides. Evey went to her room to change out of the dress and into something more comfortable. She was trying to get the zipper undone and couldn't.

Anthony happened to be walking by to go to the restroom. She was hopping around with her hands behind her back when she heard him laugh from the doorway. She turned around, red-faced.

"Would you like me to help you or just watch you hop around a little longer?" he asked, face full of amusement.

"Some help would be nice," she said to him looking at him from under her brows.

He walked over to her in a few long strides. She turned her back to him, and he let his hands slide down from her shoulders to the zipper, and he slowly unzipped her dress and let his hands rest on her hips. He was feeling warm at seeing her bra and just a sliver of her back through the crack that was now unzipped. He could also see the top of her lacy panties and had the urge to take them off with his teeth. He took a deep breath, and she leaned back into him.

"You better not. I'm not going to be able to control myself. I want to rip you out of that dress and. . . ." He looked toward the bed.

She turned to face him, now smiling, and asked, "And what?"

He shook his head and backed out of her room, slowly facing her. He did need to go to the bathroom, and with so many people in the house, it wouldn't take long for someone to find them together. He would have to finish this later. She was smiling and blew him a kiss as he walked out.

Anthony just shook his head at her and stuck his tongue out.

Evey turned around, smiling and finished taking the dress off. She didn't hear Anthony pass by the room or stop to watch her as she bent to put her shorts and slide a T-shirt on. She was beautiful, and to see her bend over in those lacy panties to put her shorts on. He was short of breath. He had to get away from her. She hung the dress back up and made her way to the kitchen.

Lunch was nice and quiet. They all ate in happy unison. The leftovers were still great and now were sided with summer squash and okra.

"So tomorrow, we will do a little fence patching and patch potholes in the road and take the old tin off the hay barn and replace it," Grandpa broke in. "If we can get those things done, we will be set to tell you bye on Tuesday."

Anthony looked up, confused.

"I guess with all the excitement, we forgot to tell you that Evey is going to come home with us Tuesday so she can help us prepare for your chief ceremony," Belle said, chuckling.

Anthony's face lit up like a Christmas tree.

"Really?" he asked, looking at Evey.

"Really. That's why we have so much to get done tomorrow, and you're going to help," Evey told him.

He nodded and said, "I think we can manage it."

After lunch, Evey told Anthony to come with so and they could go ahead and patch the road. Grandpa almost didn't allow it since it was the day of rest, but he wouldn't stop them if that's how they would manage to spend time together.

Evey went and got the little, red Honda four-wheeler out of the shed by the chicken coop and hooked up a little trailer. Anthony watched her, smiling. She could do it all and didn't ask him for help, but he would help her. He wasn't going to make her do the heavy lifting while he was there.

She drove around to the side of the utility shed to a pile of limestone and backed the four-wheeler up to it. She got off and ran across to get the old, orange Allis Chambers tractor with a bucket and scooped up a bucket full of rock and dumped it into the trailer. She told Anthony to grab the two shovels hanging in the shed, and he did and set them on top of the rock on the trailer.

"Get on," she told him, and he got on back of the four-wheeler and held on to her, laughing under his breath.

"What?" she asked.

"I just thought I would be driving you around is all," he said.

"Not today," she said as she shifted gears and went a little faster.

They went all the way to end of the mile-long road to start at the gate.

"Stay on the four wheeler, and I'll shovel," he told her.

"Anthony, I'm not letting you do that all alone. I do this all the time," she said, trying to get off the four-wheeler.

Anthony made it to her in three strides and pinned her back down to the four-wheeler and kissed her.

"You can do anything, but today, I'm here, and you're going to let me do this for you," he told her.

She smiled and shook her head, realizing he wasn't going to let her up.

"Fine," Evey said.

"Good," he smiled.

Anthony turned from her and grabbed the shovel and began to fill in the holes. He was sweating in the Texas heat. He worked for a long while and then took his shirt off. He was glistening with sweat, and Evey watched like a panther, ready to pounce on her prey. Every shovel full of rock had all his muscles contracting into a sexy array of art. She watched his back strain and his arms tighten. She must have been staring hard because he stopped and flexed for her, and she giggled and whistled at him.

They inched their way up the driveway, and he never let her lift a shovel. She got off the four-wheeler to give him a drink of water, and as she approached him, he grabbed her and rubbed his sweaty head on her.

"Ewww!" Evey screamed, laughing and trying to squirm out of his grasp.

She finally gave up because he was too strong. He bent his head to hers and placed his mouth over hers and kissed her hard. She kissed back harder. They were so into each other, they didn't notice the new Chevy truck go by.

Chapter 9

Danny was almost wrecked rubbernecking by Evey's house. She was in the middle of the driveway kissing the shirtless Indian. He all but died seeing her hands fall to his butt and squeeze. Evey had never asked him to help with the work on the farm, but he also never offered.

He felt sick. He knew they weren't together, but it didn't make it any easier to see her with him. He wasn't just driving by. He was being nosey. He supposed that was what he got for spying on her. On his way back, he pulled in. They had made it a little past halfway the drive, and he was working hard and not letting Evey help.

Evey stiffened when she turned around to see Danny pulling in. She had told him to never come near her again. Anthony gripped the shovel tighter. Surely he wasn't coming looking for a fight, Anthony thought. Danny slowed and stopped right in front of them and got out. He had no clue why he pulled in or what he was going to say.

"Anthony, I owe you an apology," Danny began. "I'm sorry for what happened at the reservation. That's really not the way I operate—my mother maybe, but not me. I can see you love Evey and make her happy, and that's all I want, for her to be happy. I wish it was with me, but I ruined that on my own."

Anthony stared at him for a long time and then looked at Evey. She looked pale.

He grabbed her hand and replied, "I appreciate your apology. Evey makes me very happy too. Our souls were linked long before we knew each other. You will have a chance at real love. Be smart enough to realize it, and you choose to be responsible and not let someone else make decisions for you. I hope you find happiness, Danny, but stay away from Evey."

Danny stiffened. He knew Anthony was a good guy but now understood he had clear boundaries. Danny looked at Evey.

She looked up to meet his eyes and said, "Danny, thank you for acknowledging you were in the wrong. It's a decent step, but you hurt me really badly, and I've let people just believe what they want to of me and our split, and that's not easy. But I won't ruin your name. However, I do ask that you keep your mother away from me and my family and let us live in peace."

He nodded and turned around and got back in his truck. There was nothing more to be said. He backed out of the drive and turned to put it in Drive. He looked in the rearview mirror to see Anthony just holding Evey and kiss her on the top of the head. He wanted that so badly.

Anthony finished patching up the holes on the driveway, and Evey went and unhooked the trailer and put the shovels up.

"Do you just want to go for a ride?" she asked him.

He smiled at her and got back on the four-wheeler.

"Okay then," she said.

She started it back up and headed toward the woods. Belle was standing in the kitchen window watching them ride off.

"Where are they going?" she asked Grandma.

"Looks like she's taking him toward the stream. There's a good place to swim back there, and it's just a nice view. In her first vision, that's where she saw Apovini working on his arrowhead," Grandma told her.

"Swimming, eh?" asked Analac, grinning.

Belle shook her head.

Evey took Anthony through a deer track and into the woods. He thought he heard water. He did. They were by a stream. She turned off the four-wheeler.

"This is where I saw in my first vision. Apovini was working on the arrowhead here," she said, grabbing the arrowhead hanging around his neck.

He smiled at her. Then she was swinging her long leg around the four-wheeler to get off. He watched her. She was taking her shirt off and slipped her shorts off. She was in her lacy bra and panties and jumped into the water.

He laughed and thought, *Well played.*

She popped back up out of the water and splashed him.

"Come on and get those pants off and get in here with me!" she demanded.

He wasn't one to tell her no, so he did as he was told and let out an Indian scream as he jumped in.

Evey swam over to him and slicked his hair back from his face. "You are a magnificent man."

He laughed and questioned, "Magnificent?"

"Oh yes. Everything about you is wonderful," she said, kissing him gently on the neck. "Mmm. You're still salty."

Evey pulled up from kissing his neck.

Anthony smiled at her and said, "My turn to taste you then."

She leaned her head back for him to kiss her neck and was surprised to feel him swim under the water and grab her panties with his teeth. He came back up with her panties in his mouth, and she squealed with excitement. After regaining his breath, he was back under the water, tasting her. She gasped and hoped he wouldn't suffocate down there but didn't want him to stop.

She was about to sink when he came back up, kissed her mouth, and told her, "You taste sweet."

She swam over to side of the stream where she could hold on to the edge, and he followed her. She put her back to edge and turned to him and pulled him to her. She was kissing him with intent. She opened her legs to him, and he came to her hard and with need. He needed to be inside her. He had seen glimpses of her all day, and he needed to have her. She wrapped her legs around him to hold on, and he ravaged her right there on the muddy side of the stream.

Evelyn was still holding on to him tight, quivering, when he pulled her chin up from his chest and kissed her slowly.

"Thank you," he said.

"For what?" she asked.

"For letting me have all of you. And I love every inch of you," he smiled.

She could tell.

"I love you too, Chief," she said, and he laughed hard, and it jolted him, still inside her. "Oh!"

"Yes," he said, starting to move within her again—this time, slowly.

He carried her out of the water and lay her on the bank and made slow, deliberate, passionate love to her. He touched and kissed every part of her. He wanted her to know his soul was hers and that he cared for her more than life itself. He hoped that he portrayed that through his body.

They lay on the muddy ground together for a long while, with her muddy head on his chest. She was listening to his heartbeat—her beat of her heart.

She kissed his chest and looked up at him.

"Anthony, I'm happy to be yours. I'm so far in now that I can't live without you."

He smiled at her and held her tight to his naked body. Finally, they managed to get up and rinsed off in the stream, air-dried for a bit, and put their clothes back on. She was on cloud nine and couldn't believe she had a man like Anthony.

Chapter 10

The next day was a busy workday. They got everything done, with Tudley on their heels. Evey appreciated having someone who would work as hard as her, and Grandpa appreciated the extra set of hands.

They finished up their chores in record time. Anthony was good with his hands and could build anything. He naturally fit in doing the work around the farm. Anthony paid attention to Evey and Grandpa. He could tell they had worked together for a long time. They just knew what the other needed. Evey would hand him tools before he even asked for them.

Anthony knew Evey would miss her grandparents while she was gone. But he had to have her with him and knew she felt the same. They got the tin taken off and replaced on the hay barn and mended a lot of fence and even worked on a few other unimportant things.

"I could get use to the extra help, Anthony," Grandpa said.

"I don't mind one bit," Anthony said.

Evey smiled seeing the two men she loved most work together and enjoy each other's company.

Grandpa sat on the porch with the women relaxing and sipping sweet iced tea with lemon. He really did appreciate the extra help and wasn't used to being done early and being able to sit down.

"Where did the kids go?" he asked the older women.

"They ran to town to get steaks," Grandma said.

Grandpa raised his eyebrows in question at her.

"We always feed anyone who helps work, and I figured we could celebrate Anthony becoming chief soon and Evey's graduation one more time before they go," she said.

"That sounds like a great idea, sweetheart," Grandpa told her, smiling.

He was surely going to miss his granddaughter once she left.

Anthony and Evey made it to the grocery store in the neighboring town. They were still in their work clothes from the day and were covered in dirt and sweat. He looked at Evey. She had on a pearl snap shirt with a white tank top underneath, blue jeans, and old dirty boots. She looked like a vision to him. Covered in dirt, she was gorgeous, and she was a hard worker. It would be nice to have her help around the reservation.

He was wearing a wifebeater shirt, jeans with a brown belt, and brown work boots, not the western type like hers though. They were a sight, and he didn't care, as long as he had her with him. They made their way into the store holding hands and talking. She grabbed a buggy right inside the door and told him to follow her. Everywhere they went, people stopped and stared. They were a dominating vision together, one dark and one light and both so tall with long, braided hair and so in love.

They made their way down the aisles and picked up salad stuff, potatoes to make baked potatoes, and then made their way to the meat section. Evey asked him if he wanted to do the honors of picking the steak, and he said he trusted her. He watched her as she picked up the ribeye steaks and gauged the thickness and marbling in them.

"This is a good one," she said, setting an inch-thick steak into the buggy.

He smiled at her and said, "That was the one I was eyeing."

She picked out the rest. They were having fun shopping together, when they turned the buggy around to suddenly face Mrs. Bailey.

"Mrs. Bailey, fancy seeing you here," Evey said coolly.

"Yes. Fancy," she replied in disgust, looking them up and down in their dirty work clothes. "I see your grandfather still has you working like a man."

"My grandfather is a smart man to teach me everything I need to know so I can do things on my own, and I love to help him. It's good for you to work every now and then," Evey replied.

"Mmm-hmm. Well, with your Indian, I figured you wouldn't need to help anymore," Mrs. Bailey said.

Evey nodded in disgust now.

"Well, Anthony is not some hired help. Unlike others, he chose to help me instead of watching me work. And you're right—he is *my Indian*," she said, reaching for his hand.

Mrs. Bailey didn't have anything to say to this. Her son wasn't one to work any extra, and to her, it was obvious the girl was in deep with this sun-kissed man. She watched the land she wanted to acquire walk away with someone who wasn't her son.

"You told her," Anthony said, chuckling.

Evey looked up at him.

"I'm your Indian, huh?" he asked playfully.

"Damn right," she said, head held high and smiling at him.

They were in line to check out. He didn't care who saw—he just bent his head and kissed her. They probably stunk from the day's work, but it didn't matter. They enjoyed even each other's smell after a hard day's work.

"I love you, and I'll be your Indian until the day I die," he told her.

"And I'll be yours," she said smiling, with her mouth still touching his.

She was his Indian too, even if her skin was pale; there was no doubting it.

Evey drove them back home, and Anthony rode with his hand on her thigh. She smiled at him. They pulled into the drive, and Evey could see the smoke already coming up from Grandpa's grill.

"I guess Grandpa is ready to eat," she laughed, nodding toward the smoke.

"Shoot, I am too. All that working today has me hungry," said Anthony.

They pulled up and made their way inside. Grandma immediately went through the bags to find the potatoes to get them baking, and Grandpa came in to season the meat. Evey put the salad stuff in the fridge and went to shower.

"Don't take forever. I need to wash up too," Anthony told her.

Evey smiled and said, "Yes dear."

Everyone laughed at their playful nature.

Chapter 11

The dinner had been delicious and filling, and Tudley loved getting steak trimmings. He was snoring under the table. Evey went straight to bed and didn't move until her Grandma was in the loft room to wake her up the next morning.

It was still dark out. Grandma wanted a moment alone with her granddaughter before she left to be with her people for the next month or so. She was nervous about her granddaughter being gone but was reassured knowing that she would be loved and looked after by three people under her roof whom she had truly come to love and see as family.

"Good morning, honey. I just wanted to sip coffee with you on the porch, just you and I, before you leave," Grandma told her, rubbing her arm to wake her.

Evey stirred and stretched and said, "That sounds wonderful. I would like to sit and just be with you before we leave."

Evey followed Grandma down the stairs and made their way to the kitchen to pour their coffee. Grandma already had it made. They went out to the old wooden rocking chairs on the porch and sat and sipped coffee and watched the sun come up together. Evey and Grandma both breathed in deep at the same time and looked at each other and smiled. Grandma took Evey's hand.

"I love you more than life itself," she told her granddaughter. "I'm so proud of you and in everything you do. Your grandpa and I did our very best with you, and though we weren't perfect, we always loved you. I'm going to miss you so much, honey. I'm happy for you that you're getting to go be with the man you love, and always support him on his journey. But selfishly, I am going to miss you. Take care of yourself and each other. Life isn't always easy, but I can see he is who you are meant to be with, and if you work together, you will be just fine. And if you choose not to come back home to Texas, it's okay. I will support whatever decision you make."

She squeezed Evey's hand with her eyes full of tears.

"Grandma, I haven't really thought that far. I can't leave you and Grandpa forever. You need me," Evey said.

"I know you would say that, and I won't deny you being here makes things easier, but you can leave us. You need to make your own path, and that path is with Anthony. You always have a place here, when you need it," Grandma said, tears falling now.

"Oh, Grandma. I love you," Evey said, getting out of her chair to kneel in front of her grandma and hold on tight to her.

Grandma knew she had to make the decision easier for her loyal granddaughter and smiled through her tears as she stroked her wild hair.

Belle and Anthony had both awaken and saw and heard the exchange from the kitchen table. Anthony tightened to see Evey feel any type of sorrow, even if it was a definite one. Belle rubbed his back.

"It will all be fine. Her grandma is a strong woman and is trying to make it easier on Evey so she doesn't feel like she has to choose because she will always choose you, son," Belle said in a quiet, sure voice to her grandson.

Evelyn tightened up and looked into her grandma's face and whispered, "Thank you."

She understood what her grandma had just done for her.

"Besides, Evey, Grandpa and I will be visiting in a month to watch Anthony take his place as chief, and you can come back and visit anytime. This farm will always be yours. Go enjoy life and put some distance between you and those who have hurt you so badly. It will be good."

And at that, she touched her granddaughter's face and stood up.

"I need to get you all a good breakfast made before you travel," she said, smiling.

Grandma did make a fabulous breakfast. She made omelets with ham, onions, and peppers, hash browns, and toast. Evey chose to sit in between her grandparents. She just needed to be by them before she left. Anthony watched her and felt a wrench of guilt for the sadness he saw in her eyes. They ate and discussed plans.

Evey then went to her room to double-check she had everything packed again, and Anthony followed her. She was checking her bag one more time when he walked in. She looked up and smiled at him.

"Evey, I'm sorry. You don't have to leave if you don't want to. I know this is your home."

"I do have to," Evey said as he looked him in the eye.

She closed in the space between them to take his face in her hands and kissed him gently.

"My home is with you, Anthony. I can't deny that," she said with confidence.

He knew she was right, but he had to let her know she had the choice.

They got all their bags packed into the red Chevy Malibu and hugged everyone again. Evey held her grandparents a little tighter and a little longer. They reassured her that everything would be fine and wanted her to go and have fun and find her place.

Belle and Analac doted on Grandpa, and he of course loved it, and then they hugged Grandma and spoke softly with her and promised to take care of their girl. Grandpa promised Evey that he would take good care of Tudley and bring him when they came in a month to see Anthony become chief. Evey loved on her coyote and promised him a nice new bed when he got to her.

Anthony got up front to drive, and Belle sat in the passenger seat. Analac and Evey sat in the back together. They pulled out, waving and blowing kisses. Anthony looked in the rearview mirror to check Evey. She looked sad but excited. She smiled at him in the mirror. Their journey was just beginning.

Chapter 12

The hours dragged on in the car. Everyone was tired from their week of excitement in Texas. Anthony was a good driver and let the ladies nap. Evey had a hard time napping. She kept watching Anthony. He was capable of caring for her, and in a short month, he would be the chief of his people.

Analac woke up to see her studying Anthony.

"What are you thinking, Pale Granddaughter?" Analac asked.

Evey smiled. She knew he was listening.

"I was thinking how he will take care of me, no matter what. I'm lucky to have him care for me, and I was thinking about how he will be chief in a month. I know he will be a great leader," said Evey.

"Indeed he will, with you by his side. Your faith in him makes him strong. Together you two are capable of anything," Analac said, patting Anthony's shoulder to make sure he was listening too.

"I know so too, Analac. Being with Evey at the farm and seeing her fix things and work with her grandpa and me, I know we can tackle all kinds of problems. I'll be a better chief, knowing she's by my side," he said, locking eyes with the women through the rearview mirror.

Analac watched the two. The thread between them was bright red and thick, almost braided. Their paths and lives were bound together more than any she had ever seen. Belle had spoken of the thread shortly after they had met, but now it was more intense to the old woman.

American Indians talked about an invisible thread that bound two souls together. For them, it is very real, and only old-timers can see the invisible red thread. Sometimes the two who are bound can feel the pull, but they can't see it. She wondered how much they felt the pull.

"Pale Granddaughter, would you hold this in your palm and see for me?" Analac asked, taking a beaded necklace with shells off of her neck, which looked really old.

"Why?" Evey asked.

"Well, this is my story, and I'd like to share it with you. I could share it in words, but for you to see it, you would know it all then. Plus, we have time," Analac said.

Evey looked at her. For Analac to want to share her story was really something. She knew she thought of her as family, but that was something else. Evey felt honored.

"Analac, grandmother of my heart, I would be honored. Would you like me to say what I see or keep it to myself?" she asked.

"It is for you to know, so you just see, and I will hold your hand to ground you," Analac said.

Evey nodded and set her hand out palm up. Analac set the old necklace in her hand and squeezed it shut with hers. Evey was instantly seeing through Analac's eyes.

She was following an old lady in the woods who was humming and laying hands on trees. Analac was a young girl.

"This way, granddaughter. The trees said it's this way," the old lady said.

They walked around to an opening by a cavern to find an herb and picked it. Then they made their way back to the longhouses.

"We need this to make the cough medicine for your parents, sweet child," the old lady spoke as she ground the plant into a bowl and poured hot water over it to steep.

Analac nodded. She heard a horrible coughing from the room. She walked toward the sound to find a couple lying in bed together, looking very ill.

"Mother, Father, we found the plant we needed to make your medicine. We will get you better," Analac said.

"Thank you, daughter," a very hoarse woman said.

But it was too late. They didn't get better. They just continued to cough and waste away. There was nothing more they could do for them, and help was hard to get on the reservation in those days. It was a slow, horrible death to watch, and she got to see it all. Her mother left her all her sewing supplies, and she went to live with her grandmother, Shine of the Moon, who was already an old woman.

Shine of the Moon taught her many things like how to sew their ceremonial clothing and how to use common herbs. She also taught her about love. Shine of the Moon's husband, Analac's grandfather, died at a young age, and Shine of the Moon never remarried. She said there was only one man who could set her soul on fire and told Analac that if a man does not set your soul on fire, then you should not be with him. She encouraged her granddaughter to find something she loved, whether it be work or man.

Shine of Moon died when Analac was sixteen. On her deathbed, she passed her gift to Analac—talking to trees. There was a song in their native tongue she had to learn:

> Tales in trees come talk to me. I promise to speak truth.
> Tales in trees come set your spirit free in me.
> Tales in trees, in ancient way your secret will stay.
> Tales in trees, I come to thee with a listening heart true.
> Tales in trees, let me see what you'd have me do.
> Tales in trees, come talk to me.

She could only use her gift for good, honest things and to help people, and she must not tell anyone of what she hears, unless it was for the greater good.

Analac did meet a man, a Navajo from a neighboring tribe, she did love very much. They began courtship and had fun together. They went bowling and to the picture show. He told her of his love for her, but tribes stayed to their own, so they courted in secret.

Then World War II came upon them, and he was drafted as a wind talker. He used his native tongue to get secret messages to other troops. They wrote letters and became extremely close in that time, but he never made it home. Analac's heart never mended, and she never married, although she did have some fun here and there. Her grandmother's words always stuck with her in her gift and about love. Analac never married or had children because she didn't feel like the love would be sufficient, but she did live a full life that was full of love. She had many friends and people whom she loved as family and a job she loved. And now, she had not a granddaughter in blood but in heart.

Evey could feel herself smiling. She opened her eyes, glistening with tears.

"Analac, grandmother of my heart, I do love you, and you are my family. Thank you for loving me and keeping my secrets. I know the tree told you," Evey said, putting the necklace back on Analac's neck.

Analac let a tear stream down her cheek but only one. She was not sad but happy to have someone acknowledge her love and their love for them.

"I love you too, granddaughter of my heart, and your secrets are always safe with me," Analac said, winking at her.

"The song—I love the song. It's beautiful. That's what you were singing at the farm by my tree. I recognized it in my seeing," Evey said.

Analac's eyes brightened at this.

"You could hear the words in your sight?" she asked.

"Oh yes, and I loved it," Evey answered. "The melody was just so sweet, and your grandmother had a nice, soft voice."

Analac had a huge toothless grin now.

"I still see her in my dreams sometimes. I'm glad you could see her too."

Anthony was in awe of their exchange in the back seat. Evey and Analac truly were family. For Analac to open her life up to her like that was something special. He wondered if she had something else up her sleeve, but for the moment, he was happy that Evey had the love of her and for her. It would help her in her transition to be the chief's woman.

Chapter 13

They made it home to the reservation with minimal stops and nothing serious to report. Evey was glad when they pulled in. She got out immediately to stretch her long legs. She walked Analac home with her bags in tow, and Anthony told her he would get her bags into his and Belle's house while she was gone. Evey did feel home. She helped Analac get settled in, and then Analac shooed her off to be with Anthony.

"I'm old, but I'm not dead," Analac told her. "I can manage. Go find your love."

Evey hugged her fiercely and told her she would see her tomorrow.

On her walk back to Belle's, Evey stopped dead in her tracks when she saw Lola. Lola was an Indian girl who didn't like Evey simply because she was with Anthony and Lola was his ex. Lola was pregnant. She looked to be midway along.

Lola stopped also when she saw Evey. Evey didn't know what to think, so she just waved at her, and Lola gracelessly waved back. Evey had to cross the street to Lola's side and really didn't want to, but she did. She was ready to get back to Belle's and be with Anthony. She made it over there and figured she might as well break the ice.

"Hi, Lola. How are you doing?" she asked.

"I'm okay. I'm a little fat, but okay."

Both girls laughed a little forcibly.

"Okay, well, it was nice to see you," Evey said.

"It's okay, Pale Granddaughter, you don't have to pretend to like me," Lola said.

Evey thought a moment and then replied, "I'm not going to pretend anything, but I will try to be friendly. We will be seeing a lot more of each other, so we might as well be cordial at least," said Evey.

Lola nodded and said, "Deal."

Evey made it back to Belle's, and she sighed when she walked through the gate. She smiled to herself as she just walked in instead of knocking. She was home.

Anthony was at the door as soon as he heard it open and had her pinned up against the door, kissing her.

"Belle?" Evey asked breathlessly.

"In the shower," Anthony said, pushing her back up against the door to kiss her again.

He finally let her catch her breath, and she looked up, smiling at him.

"I'm sure glad to be home, especially if that's the homecoming I get as soon as I walk through the door," Evey told him.

Anthony's heart skipped a beat when he heard her say *home*.

He pulled her into hug her and said, "I'm glad to have you home. I love you."

They made their way to the living room to sit down for a little while. Evey had to ask him about Lola. She was so curious. They sat down on the old, brown, floral couch, and he put his arm around her and she leaned into him and sighed.

"Beat of my heart, who got Lola pregnant? I saw her on my way back home," she asked.

"Truth is, I don't know. She hasn't said anything to anyone. It's clear to see she is carrying a child, but she hasn't come out and said it. I'm sure her parents are ashamed," he said.

"Now that you say that, when I asked her how she was doing, she just told me that she was a little fat. I hope she at least knows who the father is," Evey said.

"I hope whoever it is will step up. It's not the child's fault," Anthony said, and in that moment, Evey felt even happier that he was hers.

And she felt her heart thud thinking of Anthony as a father.

Maybe one day we could have a family of their own, Evey dreamed.

Belle came out of the shower to find the two soul mates asleep sitting up on the couch. She chuckled. She gently shook Anthony's shoulder.

"Anthony, wake up, baby. You two will be in a bind in the morning if you sleep like that," she said softly.

Anthony stirred and looked at Evey asleep on his shoulder.

"Okay. I'll get her to bed," he said sleepily.

He picked Evey up and carried her to his room and laid her in his bed and pulled the covers up to her chin and went back to the couch to lay out to sleep. He was ready for the day they could just go to bed together. He wanted to just hold her in his arms.

The next morning, Evey woke to Anthony poking her in the ribs.

"Stop it!" she hollered in between giggles.

"Nope. Get up!" he said.

"Okay, okay," she said, stretching up and pecking him on the cheek.

Evey got up and went to the bathroom to brush her teeth and get dressed. She put on blue jean shorts and a T-shirt and then made her way to the kitchen.

"Mmm, that smells great, Belle!" Evey said, looking over her shoulder to see what she was making.

"Just a breakfast stir-fry. It'll be ready in five minutes," she replied, swatting her hand away with her spoon.

Evey laughed and went and took her seat at the table by Anthony, and they ate breakfast all together.

"C'mon, I have something to show you today," Anthony told her. "We are going to get out of everyone's hair for the day so they can start planning."

"I thought I came early to help with that?" Evey asked, raised her eyebrows as she asked.

"Not today. You're coming with me," he said, grabbing her hand.

Anthony grabbed a small set of keys as they walked out the back door. Evey wondered where he was taking her. He never let go of her hand and led her through the little reservation town. Everyone stopped to wave and say hi as they walked past.

The town was buzzing with excitement for the upcoming chief ceremony, and the new couple was also a fun topic for the townsfolk. The rumors of their marriage and when they would have children were running rampant. Anthony kept walking past everybody and everything.

He led her up a narrow path to a hill through some trees. On the other side of the trees was a small wooden house on the hill. It was charming. It had wildflowers growing around it, and it looked like no one had been there in a very long time.

"This was my and my parents' house. I hadn't really thought of ever coming back here, but then you showed up. This is my house. It could be ours. I have many sad memories here, many good ones too, but I'd really like to make some new happy ones with you," Anthony said, pulling her to him.

"Anthony, I love it. It's cute, and it could be home. Are you sure?" Evey asked.

"As long as you're with me, I'm sure. Let's go check it out. We will need to do some repairs to it and paint and do updates, I'm sure. You can do anything you want," he told her, smiling as he watched her face light up.

He could see her mind working.

Evey headed up the path to the porch. Many of the boards needed to be replaced, and she could see where a flowerbed used to be around the front of it. She could envision the beds groomed and a new, white screen door open to let the fresh air in. She was smiling.

"You can see what it could be, can't you?" Anthony asked her.

"I can. I see pretty flowerbeds, a white a screen door to let fresh air in, and a porch swing just over there in that corner," she told him.

"Let's go see what needs to be done inside. I'm eager to have you to myself every night," he said, kissing her quickly.

Anthony put the little key into the door and turned the knob. When the door opened, dust flew everywhere and smelled like a house that had been shut up for a long time. Anthony went through the house to open all the windows and let fresh air in while Evey looked around. There was old furniture in the living room: a red couch, a La-Z-Boy chair, and a wooden rocking chair. She would polish that rocking chair and keep it.

The carpet was a tan color. It would have to go. She walked into the kitchen, and Anthony came in behind her. It was small but nice. It had plenty of counter space and nice cabinets. They just needed a little TLC. They would need a new stove. She was making a mental checklist. Then she realized this was where Anthony found his mother after she killed herself not being able to deal with the loss of his father in a work accident.

She looked up at Anthony and squeezed him tight around the waist.

"Are you okay, beat of my heart?" she asked him.

"I will be. I have you. I've got to let go of what was and live in what I have now," Anthony said, and he bent and kissed her and carried her out of the kitchen.

He carried her down the hallway and stopped.

"Here is the bathroom. It's a nice size. I think it just needs a good cleaning," he said, stepping in to look around.

"We can manage that," she said.

Then they walked down the hall past two small bedrooms. She could see which one was his. It had a beautiful mural painted on the wall of the hills, a stream, buffalo, deer, and rabbits, with a setting sun just in the background. Evey was speechless. It was beautiful.

"My father painted that for me when I was born and he knew he had a son," Anthony said.

"Anthony, I love it. It's beautiful. You take after him," Evey said.

They looked across the hall at the other room. It was more of a workspace. It had an old desk in it. Evey thought it would be perfect as a guest room for her grandparents. At the end of the hall was the master bedroom. It was a nice size and had a half bath attached to it. Evey wanted to paint the walls a light green in there.

"Anthony, will you paint my tree on the wall at the head of our bed?" Evey asked him.

"I would love to do that for you," he told her, smiling, as he grabbed her and kissed her.

This time, Evey let her body take over. She kissed her way down from his mouth to his neck and took his shirt off and kissed her way to his belt line. She looked up at him, and he had his eyes closed with a crooked smile on his face.

She undid his plain brown leather belt and gently slid his pants down, her hands rubbing down his rear as she did. She kissed him some more, inching her way down. She heard his breath catch when she finally and slowly took him into her mouth. She was thorough, and he ached to finish, but he wouldn't.

He lifted her chin up to look into her golden brown eyes, and he saw the love in them and knew he mirrored that love. He bent down to his knees and kissed her. He pulled at her shorts and got them undone. He pushed her down on the floor and had her right there. It didn't take long. She had already had him on the edge, but he needed all of her in that moment.

Anthony lay on top of her with his head on her chest. He loved her so much. There is something special about a soul recognizing its counterpart.

"So I take it, you like the house?" he asked, trying not to laugh.

"Yes. It's ours. When do we start to work on it?" she asked back.

"No time like the present," he said.

Anthony needed to get her in their own home so he could have her any time he wanted to. He needed to marry her first though.

Chapter 14

They did get started right away. Anthony flipped the breaker on, and then went out and found the water well and got power to the pump. It took a few minutes for everything to pressure up, but then they had water and lights. It was so exciting to them both.

Evey got working on cleaning the sinks and the bathtub and scrubbing down cabinets and toilets. Anthony worked on getting stuff out that was old and didn't work anymore. They would need to buy a bed and bedding, but they could use the bed frame and headboard. Evey was keeping a track of everything she needed in her head.

Anthony got the old furniture out of the living room and got the carpet pulled. It was a dusty mess. When he got to floor underneath, he called to Evey.

She went over to him, and he said, "I can sand, stain, and polish this wood, and we can have a wooden floor. What do you think about that?"

"I think that sounds nice and a lot cheaper than new flooring," she said, bending to kiss him.

After a few hours' work, they did all they could do for the day. They needed to get wood for the porch and a sander, stain, and polish. Anthony locked the door after they stepped out. They had a mess in the yard; old furniture, a stove, and carpet were all thrown out.

"Well, tomorrow, we will get a trailer and go get wood in town and everything else we need, and then we can load the trash up on the trailer and haul it off later," Anthony said.

"Sounds good to me," Evey replied. "Anthony, how are we going to afford all of this?"

"My parents left me insurance money that I wasn't allowed to touch until I turned eighteen. I would like to use it to set up and fix our home and to marry you," he told her, pulling her to him.

"Don't you think you should ask me first?" she asked playfully.

Anthony did in fact think he should ask her first, but how do you make something special when she knows it's coming?

They made their way back to Belle's, hand in hand, and stopped once in the little town when they bumped into Lola coming out of Analac's house.

"Lola, what are you doing at Analac's?" Anthony asked her.

"I, uh, I just needed to talk with her. I need to get a job and was hoping she would let me help her with her sewing," Lola said.

They looked at her and looked at her belly.

"Lola, are you okay?" Evey asked.

Lola's eyes filled with tears.

"Why are you so nice to me? I wasn't very nice to you," Lola said to her.

Evey took a deep breath. They fact was, she really didn't care for Lola, but she could see how Lola would want Anthony. He was perfect, and she could understand how she would want to fight for him. But Evey had Anthony, and she felt sorry for Lola; and if her parents were in fact ashamed, would she have help with the baby?

"Lola, I'm not a mean person. I understand people do things they regret, especially if they think they are losing the one they love. I've been hurt by someone who claimed to love me, I've lost my parents at a young age, and I'm blessed enough to have my soul mate. I just don't see any room for negativity. I don't want to be bitter. I know how short life can be, and I don't want to waste that time," Evey said.

Anthony looked at the woman he loved with a newfound respect.

She would be a great chief's wife, Anthony thought. *She has compassion and honesty. She would be just.*

Lola looked at her, face softening.

"You are a great person, Evelyn. You deserve him. I didn't," she said, looking down.

"But you do deserve to be loved and live a full life. So what if the first go-round didn't work? Lola, where's the father of your baby?" Evey asked gently.

Lola still hadn't come out and said it, and she just let the tears fall now.

"He nor his family want the baby," Lola strained to tell her. "They've turned their backs on me, and my parents are so ashamed of me—to be pregnant out of wedlock and to have a nonexistent father of my child. I will be okay though. Analac said she would consider hiring me to help her, she just needed to talk it over with her family first."

Evey let go of Anthony's hand and grabbed Lola into a hug.

"You don't have to it alone, Lola. We will help you where we can."

Lola burst out into crying now on Evey's shoulder, and Evey shushed and patted her back.

Finally, Lola straightened up and said, "I don't deserve your friendship."

"But you do. Anthony has opened my eyes to reservation life, and we are all one family, are we not?" Evey asked, smiling gently at the broken girl.

Anthony wrapped his arms around her at this, so proud that she was his.

"Lola, is the baby's father one of the men here?" Anthony spoke up now. "I will go talk some sense into him."

She stiffened and said, "No, he's not one of us. I had a moment of weakness in a bad state of mind and slept with someone once, and well, here I am."

He nodded.

"Well, you heard Evey. If you need anything, we will do what we can to help you. You are one of my people," he said, grabbing her arm in reassurance, and they parted ways.

Analac was standing in her doorway in front of her screen door. Analac never ran the AC, so she had heard it all and was proud of the young couple.

Yes indeed, they would be great leaders, Analac thought.

"Evey, Anthony!" she yelled from her doorway.

They both turned to smile at her.

"Hey, Analac. How are you today? Are you rested from our trip?" Anthony asked, eyeing her.

"Oh yes indeed. I see you saw Lola here. Would you two come inside a moment and let me speak with you?" Analac asked.

"Sure," Evey said, heading toward the door and pulling Anthony along.

He really was ready to shower and relax after all the demo work, but he followed.

"I heard what you said to Lola. I'm very proud of you. And when Lola said that I told her I needed to talk to my family first, I was referring to you both," Analac said.

Anthony and Evey looked at her in surprise and full of love.

"I know that three of you have a rocky past," Analac continued. "I would like to help her but not at risk of hurting either of you. I love you both."

"Oh, Analac, you are too good to us. We love you, and we would never stand in your way to help someone," Evey said, grabbing Anthony's arm.

"She's right. We are glad you want to help Lola. She seems to be in a real hard spot. A job would help her have purpose," Anthony added.

Analac smiled her big toothless smile.

"You kids were wonderful. You are both smart beyond your years, and you will lead our people well. I will tell Lola to be at the house in the morning to get started," Analac said to them and hugged them both.

They both breathed a sigh of relief when they walked into Belle's house. She was cooking dinner. It smelled wonderful. Anthony went straight to the bathroom for a shower. Evey had the urge to follow him in but didn't. Soon enough, she could do whatever she wanted with him when they were in their own home. She went into the kitchen to see if Belle needed help.

"Hey, daughter. How was your day?" Belle asked.

"It was very good—very busy but good," Evey replied.

She filled Belle on all—well, almost all—of the day's events, from the house to Lola admitting she is pregnant, to Analac asking them if she could hire Lola.

Belle smiled and nodded. "You two made good choices. Anthony's father and grandfather would be so proud. To be good leaders, you have to care about your people more than yourself, and you did that today by putting pride aside and helping Lola."

"I can't imagine having a baby without the support of my family," Evey said.

Belle sighed and nodded in agreement.

They ate dinner and made plans for the next day. Anthony would go to town to get supplies to work on the house, and Evey would go with Belle to help Analac design the ceremonial outfits for Anthony becoming chief and figure out the menu. Then she would go out to the house to help Anthony.

Belle was happy that they would be living in the house her son had built, and to know her grandson was now working on it made her heart fill with sorrow, love, and pride. Everyone went to bed, but Anthony followed Evey to his room and climbed in bed with her.

"What are you doing?" she asked him.

"I'm going to bed. What do you think I'm doing?" he asked her back with a slight smile on his face.

"What about your grandmother? I don't want to disrespect her in her home," Evey said.

"I talked with her while you were in the shower. I'm sure she knows that we don't just hang out all the time and we are working on our home so we can move in together, and plus, I'll sleep much better in my bed," he said, nuzzling her.

"As long as she's okay with it, I'm happy to be able to share a bed with you," she said, giggling and turning over to hold him close to her, and in two breaths they were both sound asleep.

Belle woke up first the next morning, and she peeked in Anthony's room and smiled. The two were a tangle of covers and legs. They both had long legs. Anthony slept with one foot out of the cover. He was holding Evey close to him, his leg in between hers, and Evey was asleep with her mouth wide open. Belle chuckled.

Anthony woke up to see his grandmother in his doorway, smiling. He raised an eyebrow in inquiry, and she just nodded toward Evey. He suppressed a laugh. He and Evey were a tangled-up mess, and her hair was all over the place and her mouth was open. He rubbed her hair back off her face, and she grunted. Both Anthony and Belle laughed out loud at that.

Evey sat, bolt upright.

"Good morning," she said, feeling embarrassed. "Was I sleeping badly?"

"Oh, no, you were sleeping well. Your mouth was just wide open," Anthony said, laughing.

"Gee, thanks y'all for making fun of me in my delicate state," she said, playing around.

Evey got up and got dressed. She went to the living room and called her grandparents. She did miss them but was so happy with Anthony.

"Hello?" Grandpa said in his deep voice.

She always wondered why men used a much deeper voice to answer the phone.

"Hey, Grandpa," Evey said, sounding bright as the sun.

"Evey! How are you doing, sister?" he asked, not hiding his joy at hearing her voice.

"I'm doing well, enjoying my time so far! Anthony showed me a house yesterday that's his. We started working on it to clean and fix it up. It was his parents'," Evey was telling him.

"Hey, Honey! Did I hear you have a house?" Grandma busted in on the phone.

Evey filled them in on the house and what they were working on.

"Well, sister, I guess you two better get married soon if you're planning on living together," Grandpa said.

"I guess so," Evey echoed him.

She filled them in on Lola and Analac and told them they will would be working on planning the ceremony today. They hung up with reluctance and many I love yous.

Chapter 15

Anthony headed off to town in his old Ford F-150 with a lowboy trailer ready to go get supplies for their house. Evey went with Belle and walked across to Analac's house to start designing ceremonial outfits. Belle and Evey were going to work on jewelry, while Analac did the sewing. They made it to Analac's door, and Belle did a rhythmic knock and walked on in.

"We are in the sewing room!" Analac hollered toward the door.

Evey and Belle made their way back there to see Lola helping Analac. She was cutting leather for Analac.

"Good morning, ladies," Evey said to both of them.

"Good morning, Daughter! I've already started on your dress. I still have your measurements, so I started."

"Yay, thank you Analac!" Evey said with happiness.

"Good morning, Evelyn," Lola said with almost a smile."

"Lola, you may call me Evey if you want," Evey told her, smiling, making a real attempt to be kind.

Lola smiled at her.

"Analac, where would we best help? Stringing beads for the jewelry?" Belle asked.

"Yes, Belle. I've got everything laid out on the table by the window for you," Analac explained.

Evey and Belle went and sat down and started to put the colorful beads onto the thin jewelry wire. Analac and Belle started singing a song in their tongue, and Evey smiled as she looked down and worked. It was a beautiful song. It helped them get the work going.

"Ah. Daughter, come here," Analac said sometime later.

She was holding up a beautiful Indian dress. It was a blond leather with royal blue and white material on the top at the sleeves to bind each side together. On the front it had tiny royal-blue-and-white beading across the front of the chest of the dress and, at the bottom, more beading to match and fringe. She loved it.

"This is gorgeous, I love it!" Evey exclaimed.

Analac smiled. "I knew you would like the beading."

Lola watched the two women with a longing deep in her gut. She wished she had relationships like that. She was jealous but, this time, held no malice.

Evey noticed Lola watching them and tried to include her, "What do you think, Lola?"

"I think it's a gorgeous dress," she said.

"What are you going to wear, Lola?" Evey asked.

"Oh, I'm not going to go. I don't have anything proper or that fits with this melon in my belly," she said, softly laughing.

"Nonsense. You will go with me, and you will make yourself a dress," said Analac.

Lola's whole face brightened.

"Yes, you cannot miss this, Lola. This is history and will be good for the baby to know," Belle said.

Analac looked to Belle now.

"Lola's parents are throwing her out because she is with child of a man who is not of our people and wants nothing to do with the baby. I'm going to let her live here. I cannot bear to think of a young pregnant girl with nowhere to go," Analac said.

"I'd have to say I agree with you, and Lola is a very lucky girl to have you," Belle replied, looking at Lola. "We take care of our own, Lola. You and your baby will always have somewhere to stay. Anthony and Evey will be moving out of my house before too long, and I will have room too if you need it."

Lola's eyes filled with tears. "You owe me nothing, yet you give to me. I don't know how to thank you."

"Live a good, full life and be a good mother to your child. Remember where you come from and who has helped you as you go on your way," Analac said, and Belle nodded in agreement.

Evey was happy to be in the presence of such great women.

She continued working on a huge beaded necklace. It would be for Anthony to wear. It was a big ceremonial piece. Analac used blue and white beads to match Evey's dress. Evey wondered what his outfit would look like. Analac was working on it now. She tried not to wonder too much on the father of Lola's baby, but she just couldn't imagine someone not wanting to be a part of their child's life.

It's not the baby's fault, and for goodness sake, that child would be part of you! Evey ranted to herself, looking at Lola, and Lola actually smiled at her.

Lola had relaxed now knowing she had a place to live.

At five o'clock, Analac announced that that was enough work for the day and her fingers were tired. Belle and Evey hugged her and Lola goodbye.

When they got home, she noticed Anthony still wasn't back.

"I'm going to walk to the house to check on him," Evey told Belle.

"Yes, you go do that, and I'll heat up the leftovers. They'll be ready whenever you come in," Belle told her.

Evey went out the back door to head out to the edge of the reservation to her house on the hill. She smiled when she got to the other side of the trees and saw the house with Anthony's truck and the trailer loaded with the trash. He had really been working hard.

Evey was shocked when she got to the porch. He had already replaced all the boards that needed to be, and in the corner was a swing. He had built her a swing and hung it already. She was speechless. She had no idea how he worked so fast. She walked in the house to find him on hands and knees sanding the floor. He looked up to her and smiled. He was filthy and had tiny bits of wood all over him.

"You have been really busy," she said to him.

"Yes I have. It looks like a mess now, but these floors will be pretty. The wood grain is real nice on it, and I went ahead and did the whole house," he said pointing, toward the hall.

She looked down the hall. He had sanded the entire house! She saw the shop vac in the kitchen. She went over to it, got it, and went down the hall to start vacuuming up the sawdust. He watched her go, and once again, he was thankful for her and how she didn't mind to work. He didn't even have to ask her. She saw what needed to be done and just did it.

After she finished vacuuming, she went over to Anthony and hugged him tight.

"I can't believe you already built me a swing. You are amazing," she said and got up on her toes to kiss him.

"You are worth it," he said, winking at her.

"Oh, and dinner is ready. Your grandmother was heating up leftovers as I walked over here. She's probably wondering where we are at," Evey said, feeling guilty for taking so long.

Anthony raised an eyebrow and said, "She knows where we are. She's probably wondering what we're doing."

"Anthony!" Evey shrieked.

"What? It's the truth," he teased.

They walked out the door and onto the porch.

"At least go try out the swing before we leave," he told her.

Evey walked over to it and sat down and gently pushed back with her feet and closed her eyes. He watched her with a smile on his face.

"What are you thinking?" he asked her.

"I'm thinking about sitting here in this swing with a baby one day and rocking him or her to sleep, and then I'm thinking about sitting on this swing with you when we are old and rocking our grandchildren," she said, opening her eyes and smiling at him.

"Good, because I can see that too," he said to her.

Anthony asked her all about her day on their way back to Belle's. She told him all about Lola and the beautiful dress Analac already finished for her and the necklace she was working on for him. He smiled to see her so excited to work with the other Indian women.

"Evey, how do you feel about opening the clay pot we dug up in Texas?" Anthony asked.

The clay pot had Apovini's and Pale Daughter's precious belongings in it.

"I'm okay with that, Anthony. I would like for you to have the feather's out of it for your headdress. One of them was Apovini's and the other was the first chief's that he gave to Sarah, and I'll use the one that was just Sarah's in my hair," she said, thinking aloud.

He smiled at her.

"The feathers are great, but I was thinking more along the lines of the ring in there that Apovini made for Pale Daughter. I would like to put it on your finger, if you'll allow me to," Anthony said, stopping in the middle of the path to face her and look into her eyes.

She got up on her toes and pulled him down to her and kissed him passionately.

With their faces still touching, Evey said, "I would like nothing more than the world not to question I am yours. Put the ring on my finger."

They made it back home to Belle's, and she was waiting in the living room for them.

"I heard you two made quite the spectacle in the middle of the street," she said, eyebrows raised.

"I'm sorry Belle. It was a moment of passion," Evey said.

"I'm not sorry for kissing my wife in the street," Anthony said.

Belle and Evey both looked at him as he chuckled.

"I asked Evey if I could put Pale Daughter's ring on her finger, and she said yes. In my eyes, you"—he looked at her—"are already my wife."

Belle clasped her hand to heart and let a tear fall down her cheek and got up and came to them and hugged them both.

"So when will we have a wedding ceremony? Before you move into the house surely?" Belle was asking, gearing up to start planning.

She loved to plan a good party, but first things first, she went and got the clay pot out of her herb room.

Chapter 16

Anthony called Evey's grandparents while she was in the shower. "Hello, Ermis residence," Grandma answered.

"Hi, Grandma. It's Anthony. I was hoping to talk to you and Grandpa, if I may," Anthony said.

"Sure, dear. Let me just get him," Grandma said. "Okay, we are both here now."

"I'm calling because I wanted to get your blessing. I would very much like to marry Evey, and I know that you two mean the world to her, and we have to have your support. I love her more than life itself and will do whatever I have to, to keep her happy and safe," Anthony said.

He heard Grandma's breath catch. She was filled with emotion, so Grandpa answered for them both.

"Son, we know you will. That's why we let her go with you already. In our eyes, you are already our family. She is our pride and joy, and all we want for her is to be happy and be with the one she loves most," Grandpa said. "So we will get Tudley brought to you as soon as we can get there."

They all laughed. Leave it to Grandpa to make a joke out of anything.

"Anthony, we are honored to have you love our granddaughter. Take care of her," Grandma broke in now. "Have you discussed when you will have the wedding?"

"That's the thing, I'm not sure. But I was hoping maybe you could help me with that. With you two already coming in a couple weeks, I thought maybe we do it while you're already here," Anthony said.

"Two weeks is awfully fast, but we can do it. I'll call Analac later. Let me talk to Belle please. Oh, and love you, sweetie," Grandma added quickly.

"Love you too," he said, laughing.

Belle was sitting across him smiling and reached her hand out for the phone.

"Hi, Dottie! We will officially be family soon!" Belle said.

Then they were planning a wedding. He hoped Evey wouldn't mind too much.

"Don't worry about the dress. Analac has been working on it since she the two of them danced together the first time. You just bring whatever you feel is important. Oh, flowers would be nice," Belle said, as Anthony walked out as the two ladies continued to talk.

He needed to catch Evey in the hall and hold her tight to him.

Evey turned the water off in the shower. She was smiling. She was going to get married. She looked at her left ring finger, trying to imagine the ring made out of bone on it. She would wear it and be proud of it for Sarah. She dried off and slipped on cotton shorts and a tank top. She was ready to eat and relax.

She opened the door to find Anthony waiting for her. She smiled at him with the towel still on top of her head. He smiled at her too and in an instant was pulling the towel off her head and pulling her into him, his mouth ready to receive hers.

She gasped when he let his hand run up her cotton shorts. He put hand over her mouth and continued his work. Evey squirmed under his weight that now had her pushed up against the wall. He knew his grandmother would be on the phone at least an hour to talk about the wedding. He took his hand from her shorts and pushed her back into the bathroom. She eyed him.

"Your grandmother?" Evey questioned out of breath.

"She'll be busy for a while. We'll just be quiet," he said, smiling at her knowingly like someone who was about to catch their prey.

He tore her shorts down and bent her over the sink. She gasped as he rushed into her.

"Shh," he said to her as he slowed into her.

He was thrusting so hard and fast, she could hardly catch her breath. She looked up into the mirror above the sink and saw his strong hands holding her waist and his arm muscles tense as he pulled her back into him. She looked up to catch his eyes in the mirror, and he lost it.

He laughed quietly with his head on her back and then grabbed her towel to clean up.

She was laughing and said, "What was that all about?"

"I called your grandparents and got their blessing. They are happy for us," Anthony said, smiling so big his face hurt.

"You did?" She asked deliriously happy, her eyes lit up.

"I did. And now our grandmothers are planning a wedding. That's why I came and stole this time with you," he said.

"I hardly call it stolen time. I was willing to give it to you," she said, laughing. "Wait, they are planning a wedding?"

"I was thinking that since your grandparents will be here in two weeks, we might as well do it while they are here," he said.

"Oh my gosh. I have to figure out what I'm going to wear," Evey said, and then Anthony cut her off.

"Grandmother told yours that Analac has been working on a dress for you since we first danced together. I guess she was positive then that we were meant to be together," he said, smiling.

"Leave it to Analac to be ready. I'll ask her about it tomorrow," Evey said, feeling the excitement rise up in her.

When Evey went into the living room, Belle and Grandma were still talking. Belle was telling her how amazing Evey was to treat Lola the way she did and how she felt sorry for the poor girl.

Evey just smiled at her.

"Speaking of the devil, she just walked in. I'll let you congratulate her," Belle said, handing Evey the phone.

"Hey, Grandma!" Evey said full of excitement.

"Hey, honey! Your grandpa and I are so happy for you. We can't wait to be there to celebrate with you in person. You are going to be the most beautiful bride," she said, and Evey could hear the tears in her voice.

"Thank you, Grandma. I love you," Evey said.

"I love you too, honey. See you soon!" Grandma said and they hung up.

Anthony was leaning on the doorway, smiling at her. He got the gist of their conversation.

They finally made their way to the kitchen to eat leftovers. They were famished.

Anthony looked up to Evey from across the table and asked her, "Do you want to open the pot now or later?"

Evey thought for a moment.

"How about we open it at your ceremony and we announce our wedding when you place the ring on my finger and I announce my loyalty to my chief by placing the feathers in your hair?" she said, thinking as she spoke.

"Daughter, that is the most wonderful idea. It'll be a first and our people will love that! Two celebrations in one!" Belle exclaimed, pleased with Evey's idea.

Anthony smiled at her and said, "You will be the best chief's wife. No offense, Grandmother. I'm proud to call you mine."

Evey turned red and smiled at him and noticed Belle was smiling too. They were all happy.

"Oh, I've got to call Analac," Belle said, hurrying to the living room.

There was a bunch more excitement on the line, and Anthony and Evey ate in happy companionship. In a few short weeks, that would be their normal—the two of them together all the time.

Chapter 17

The days passed by quickly with all the preparations for the ceremony. The wedding was kept very hush-hush so it would be a surprise at the ceremony. Evey was proud of the necklace she had made, and she couldn't wait to place it on Anthony's neck. He had been busy working on the house and prepping his speech and just getting ready to take everything on being chief entailed.

Lola had gotten settled in at Analac's and was very happy there and happy to be learning a trade. She turned out to be good at sewing. Her maternity ceremonial dress turned out nicely. She liked fringe. She and Evey had almost become friends. They learned to like each other, and Lola couldn't say anything bad of Analac's granddaughter of her heart.

Evey would finish up helping the ladies and then walk to the house to see what she could help Anthony with. He was brilliant with his hands and great with woodwork. In a few days, he had the wooden floors done. They turned out beautifully. He repolished the rocking chair, and Evey made a colorful striped pillow for it. She planned on rocking in that chair. Anthony's mom had rocked him in that chair as a baby. He couldn't wait to see his wife holding their baby in that chair someday.

Evey hung a new shower curtain. It was a plain white material curtain with bunched-up areas every so often, and she got a white, fluffy bath rug. She said her grandma said white towels were smart because she could just bleach them. He didn't argue. He was just happy to see her happy.

She set off to painting the kitchen light yellow and the cabinets a cream color, which looked nice. Belle bought them red pots and pans as a wedding gift but said they couldn't have them until after the wedding. Belle and Evey decided pops of red would look good in a yellow kitchen.

Anthony didn't care. They didn't have a dining table yet. He would make one when he had time. Analac made them Aztec-print curtains for the living room and pillows to match for the couches they would hopefully get soon. Evey didn't touch the living room walls. They were wooden and looked like a cabin, and she liked it. She said she would get a Ficus tree to brighten up the space. He laughed thinking about all the things she thought of that he could care less about. He just needed her home with him. The rest were just details.

Evey made it to one room at time. She went into Anthony's old room. She wanted the mural to stay for their child one day. It would be fine for a boy or girl, with the right decorations. She was in there studying the room, when a sweaty Anthony came up behind her and put his arms around her.

"What do you want to do in here?" he asked.

"I think I'm going to put a fluffy area rug in the middle and move the rocking chair to the corner in here by your old dresser. I am going to paint the dresser and add new knobs to it. It'll bring it back to life, and I'll put a little lamp on top. I want to keep the mural. Maybe we can figure out how to brighten it back up. Clear coat, maybe? The rest of the walls, I'm thinking cream. You can add anything to cream. I'm not really sure what else just yet. It'll depend on if we have a boy or girl first when we start our family," she said, smiling up at him.

"I think that sounds wonderful," he said, kissing the top of her head.

They had never had the baby discussion, but they both wanted children. He smiled envisioning it.

The next room was the one across the hall. She decided to paint it cream too, and they would keep it as an office but they would add a futon so it could double as a guest room. She polished the old desk up and loved it. There was a nice wooden chair with it too. Anthony said his grandfather had made it.

The last was their room. Evey painted the walls light green and repolished the wooden bedframe and head and footboards. They had flowers carved into them.

Once she finished painting, Anthony came in and looked at it and said, "It looks nice. The color has a calming effect. As soon as I finish working on the roof and get my mess cleaned up, I'll get to the tree, but it may be after we are married and move in. I'm sorry about that, Evey."

"Oh, Anthony, I'm not worried about that at all. I love working on our home together, and it will be a work in progress until the day we die. I'm just happy to have a home with you," she said.

The last little thing to worry about was their half bath. She found a bath rug with a tree on it and toothbrush and soap holders with trees. She put an ivy in the windowsill. Their room started feeling like home.

Anthony took her to town the next day to pick out a mattress, futon, couch, and a chair. This stuff was expensive. They decided against buying a table. Anthony could make one. They pulled into the furniture store with the trailer empty. That must have set the salespeople's radars off because they flocked to them as soon as they walked in.

Anthony politely told them they were definitely planning on leaving the store with furniture but to let his bride browse for what she wants first and then they'll come get someone. Evey was glad to have him with her to take care of things like that.

They sat on every couch, and he kissed her on every couch too, saying, "You have to make sure it feels right while I'm kissing you."

"You would say anything to steal a kiss, wouldn't you?" Evey asked, giggling.

"I won't deny it, but hey, if it works." He shrugged, reaching in quick to steal a peck.

Evey laughed. They ended up picking out a tan-colored couch on which Analac's handmade pillows would look good, and it just so happened they could get the matching La-Z-Boy for 50 percent off with the purchase of the couch. Then they picked a futon. They picked one with a wooden frame and navy-blue-and-white-striped cushion.

Lastly, they needed a mattress. Their bedframe was a queen size. She had wanted a king, but queen meant they would sleep closer together. They lay on many of the mattresses, with Anthony rolling on top of her to make sure the mattress was still comfortable with his weight on top of her. Evey giggled and blushed.

The salespeople just stared at them. They ended up picking a really soft pillow top, and they got complimentary pillows with the mattress and box spring purchase.

The furniture store employees were shocked to see two very young people purchasing so much. Anthony paid them in cash. He let them know that they were soon to be married and they were getting their house ready. They smiled and could care less as long as he was paying. They loaded the futon into the back of his truck and carefully loaded everything else up on the trailer. They told Belle not to worry about cooking that night as they would pick up a few pizzas in town to celebrate.

They made their way home slowly, and Anthony drove out to their house on the hill. Evey was surprised to see her grandparents' truck parked outside their house.

She jumped out of the truck and ran toward the door, but Tudley met her before she made it. She was rolling on the ground with him and loving on him, telling him how she missed him, and then the dog darted toward Anthony to give him the same treatment.

The door flung open, and her grandma was bounding down the steps. Evey made it to her in a few steps and swooped her grandma up into a fierce hug. Then Grandpa was right there, holding them both in a hug.

"I didn't know you were coming early! You weren't supposed to be here for a few more days!" Evey said, smiling ear to ear.

"Well, we couldn't wait, and Grandma wanted to be here for wedding planning, and I wanted to bring you your wedding gift," Grandpa said.

Anthony made his way to them and was being hugged fiercely by Grandma.

"Come in and see what we brought," Grandpa said.

Evey followed him in to find a beautiful farmhouse-style dining table.

"Grandpa, it's perfect," Evey said with tears coming to her eyes, knowing his work when she saw it.

"I started working on it after you left, assuming you would need one sooner or later. With all the work you and Anthony got done for me, I had plenty of time," Grandpa said, smiling.

It was a nice size table with a bench seat on one side, two captain's chairs, and two regular chairs.

"I love it, thank you," she said hugging Grandpa's neck.

"Whew. That is one nice table. Thank you so much," Anthony said.

Anthony ran and got the pizzas and drinks and set them out on their new table where they promptly ate. Grandpa then helped Anthony get the new furniture inside. Evey gave her grandma the tour. Grandma loved everything, and her breath caught in her throat when she saw Anthony's old room. It was clear they were leaving it as a child's room.

"The mural is breathtaking," Grandma said, squeezing Evey's hand.

"My son painted that," Belle said, walking into the room with a sad smile on her face. "I'm glad it'll be enjoyed again."

Grandma hugged Belle. She could tell she needed it.

Grandma smiled seeing the white towels. She knew why Evey would get those. Then she walked into their room. The walls were a nice light green. She had brought Evey her patchwork quilt for her bed, and as soon as Evey got the new mattress in there, she put on her green sheets and pillows and put the quilt out on the bed. It looked beautiful with the green walls. Grandma looked over to see a tiny bed on the floor that mirrored the big bed.

"What is that?" she asked.

Evey laughed. "Oh, Anthony made Tudley his own bed."

She whistled for Tudley who came bounding in and noticed the bone on his little bed right away, and lying down and chewing right away. Grandma smiled again when she saw the little trees in their small bathroom. Evey would always have to have a piece of home with her, which reminded her of the picture of her tree.

Grandma reached into her pocket and grabbed the four-by-six photo out and handed it to her. Evey smiled and sat it on the dresser. She showed her grandma the office and explained how that would be the guest room with the futon.

"But this time, they'll be staying with me," Belle broke in. "You and Anthony will stay here together."

Evey smiled at her. She appreciated this gesture. She supposed no one really wants to be within earshot of newlyweds. Evey's home was almost complete with handmade touches throughout her home. They just needed appliances now. She was so happy. and so was Anthony.

They were home—in their home—and free to make their own memories.

Chapter 18

Anthony and Evey stood in their doorway and waved goodbye as the old folks left to go to Belle's. They stood for a moment longer after watching them leave and just looked at each other then smiled. Their first night in their home, all alone—almost alone, that is. Tudley came running past them to go outside and run.

"I've got both my boys home with me. I'm one happy girl," Evey told Anthony, smiling as she watched Tudley run through the trees.

He squeezed her tight and walked over to the porch swing. She followed him and sat down and sank into him with a sigh. They slowly swung back and forth as they watched Tudley play. Life was so good.

When they went in, Evey was ready for a shower. They had towels but no clothes. They weren't planning on moving in today. She laughed out loud, and Anthony looked at her, puzzled.

"I hope you're excited to hang out in your birthday suit with me. We don't have any clothes here yet," she said, laughing.

"I wasn't planning on wearing clothes anyway," Anthony laughed, slapping Eve's behind as she walked away to take a shower.

Evelyn got the water just right and stepped in. She liked her water hot. It felt good after their day filled with surprises and fun. She heard the door open, and she smiled. Her groom was coming to join her.

He opened the shower curtain to find her, head tilted back and rinsing the soap from her hair. The water and suds cascaded down her body, and he went stiff for her. She opened her eyes to find him staring. She smiled at him. He smiled back and pulled his clothes off. She watched him.

He jumped in the shower and screamed like a girl.

"Holy shit! Evey, you're going to burn my skin off. That water hurts," he said, retreating to back side of the tub.

"I'm sorry, Anthony," Evey laughed. "I like the water hot. I'll cool it off for you. I'm almost done. I'll get out of your way."

"No, I don't want you to leave me in here alone. I want to wash and touch you and let our bodies slip with the water," he said to her.

"Anthony, your water is cold!" she shouted.

He laughed then.

"I'm going to get out and dry off. You can find me in our bed when you get out. I'll be ready for you," she said, kissing him on the cheek, trying not to get in his water.

"I guess that will be fine," he said.

Evey did dry off, and she dropped her towel in the hall on the way to their bedroom. She was smiling. It would be nice to have him in a bed. Outside and impromptu lovemaking was fun but sometimes left bruises in unexpected places. She laughed thinking about the bruise she had on her backside from the floor.

Tudley was fast asleep on his new bed, bone under his chin.

You just stay that way, Evey thought, smiling.

Then she went to her bed and lay on her belly on top of the covers, waiting for Anthony.

Anthony's breath caught in his throat when he saw her lying on her stomach with her feet bent up in the air. He had seen her towel in the hall and knew she would be naked. He dropped his towel at the end of the bed. She turned her head to see him and smiled.

"Stay like that," he told her, and he slowly made his way up her body.

He started kissing her feet, kissed his way up her legs, and stopped to give adequate attention to her honeypot. Evey moaned, and it made him move his tongue faster. Then he kissed her bare butt and up her back until he was directly over her.

Anthony kissed her neck and then her mouth, and as he kissed her mouth, he parted her thighs and slid himself in. She arched up to meet him, and he let out a little moan. She smiled at that. They'd never had each other that way or in a bed, and it was brilliant. Without the fear of someone interrupting them, they took their time. He had her every way possible, driving her into ecstasy over and over. Their bodies were so in tune with each other. A touch would send sensations throughout their entire bodies. They knew that was them truly being one and enjoyed every second of it.

Evey curled into him and fell right asleep. She was still tingling all over and felt lightheaded after their lovemaking, and Anthony felt pretty good about himself too. He cradled her naked body next to him and fell asleep with his world in his arms.

At some point in the middle of the night, Evey woke up to Anthony kissing her neck and parting her legs to touch her. She sighed and flipped over so he could reach what he was searching for, and she reached down for him and rubbed slowly. He let out a sigh and let his head fall on her shoulder. She giggled.

He must be dreaming, Evey thought.

Evey woke early the next morning with Anthony's arm wrapped firmly around her and him breathing on her neck. She smiled. She quietly slid out from under him and grabbed her towel off the floor to wrap herself up and let Tudley out to potty. She sat on the porch swing and watched the sun come up.

The sun warmed her from the inside out, and she closed her eyes and breathed the moment in. She would remember that moment her whole life. Then she looked over to the doorway to see Anthony standing there in all his glory watching her.

"What are you doing?" she asked.

"Watching the most beautiful woman in the world take the morning in. God, Evey, you are beautiful, and I love you," he said to her.

"I know you love me. You show me over and over, and, Anthony, I love you too," Evey said, smiling at him.

"I woke up when I realized you weren't by me anymore. I have to say I sleep better with you by me," he said.

"Isn't there some Indian saying for that?" Evey asked.

"There's an Indian saying for everything," he laughed. "The one that comes to mind though is the legend that says when you can't sleep at night, it's because you are awake in someone else's dream. And I suppose that can't be true because I still dream of you, even with you in my arms, and it seems you sleep right through."

"I'm not sure if I sleep right through your dreams. I was woken up by your touching while you were dreaming. It seems your dreaming of me does keep me awake," she said.

He smiled a big smile and made his naked way over to her, and she giggled.

They were kissing on the porch swing, and he had just pulled her towel off her and was getting in place to get on top of her when they heard someone clear their throat.

Evey looked up, startled. Anthony quickly took the towel and covered both their bottoms and positioned himself in front of Evelyn so whoever it was wouldn't see her bare chest. It was Lola.

"Umm. Good morning, Lola," Anthony said, choking a little.

Evey was bright red and looking over his shoulder.

"Good morning, you two. I guess I can't unsee that," Lola said, snickering under her breath.

"Do you need something? Is everything okay?" Evey asked now.

"Everything is fine, but your grandparents realized that you wouldn't have any clothes here after they got back last night, and seeing how you didn't come to get any . . . well, they thought they should probably send me over with some fresh clothes for you, and I guess it's a good thing they sent me," she said, now laughing out loud.

"I guess so. Uh, you can just give them to me," Anthony said, not moving but reaching his hand out.

Lola walked up the steps and handed him the bag of clothes.

"Lola, you won't mention this to anyone, will you?" Evey asked, worried.

"I won't say a word," she said smiling and turned and walked off.

Evey let her head fall on Anthony's shoulder. She could feel he was laughing.

"What are you laughing about?" she asked, feeling annoyed.

"Poor Lola. I think she got a good look at my backside. I imagine it's not that great of a view when I'm going to straddle someone," Anthony said.

Evey started to laugh, imagining it from Lola's view.

"Oh, Anthony. That's terrible," she said in between gasps.

"Now where were we?" Anthony said as he threw the towel on the ground and pounced on top of her.

Chapter 19

Anthony and Evelyn walked hand in hand to Belle's, with Tudley following close by. The townsfolk watched them warily with the coyote in tow.

Evey waved and told everyone, "His name is Tudley, and he is friendly."

But the townsfolk nodded suspiciously.

Evey and Anthony were feeling exuberant after the night they had and after the morning too. They walked in the front door to the smell of bacon and coffee. Evey went straight to the coffeepot.

"Long night?" Grandpa asked.

Evey felt the blood rush to her face.

"No, but we don't have a coffee pot, and I'm having withdrawals," she said, smiling.

Anthony kissed his grandmother on the cheek.

"Thanks for sending Lola with some extra clothes this morning," he said, shooting a glance at Evey who smiled into her coffee cup.

Tomorrow was the big chief ceremony, so Grandpa told Anthony he would help him do whatever needed to be done. They would be setting up tents and getting wood for the great fire and smoking meats. The women would make sure the sides were made, the clothing was all the way ready, and little centerpieces done. And on a side note, Analac's ninety-fifth birthday was in a few short days as well. Belle and Grandma would be sure to celebrate her.

Evey stole off to Anthony's room to grab their clothes to take to their house.

Our house, she smiled with the thought.

She packed all her clothes back up and all she could fit of his into the two suitcases she had brought.

"I'm going to run the clothes home right quick, and then I'll meet you at Analac's," she hollered as she went out the back door.

Grandma smiled and said, "Well, she's just right at home, isn't she?"

"I sure hope so because she makes life so much better," Anthony spoke up.

"Anthony, let's get to it," Grandpa grunted and was full. "We're losing daylight."

Anthony smiled and nodded and got up from the table. He and Grandpa headed off to set up tents.

Evey made her way through the town with Tudley and the suitcases. Lola spotted her and walked over.

"Would you like some help, Evey?" Lola asked.

Evey smiled and said, "Actually, that would be great, but should you be pulling it?"

Lola grabbed one of the suitcases and laughed, "I'm pregnant, not disabled!"

Evey laughed too.

"Thank you, Lola, for helping and for, um, this morning," Evey said, looking away.

Lola smiled again. "You know, Indians have a different way of thinking about sex than most people. No one will look down on you here, as long as you don't get pregnant out of wedlock. You and Anthony are clearly made for each other. Even I have to admit it."

Evey thought a moment and then said, "Lola, thank you. I know you care for him, and it can't be easy for you."

"It wasn't at first, but even I have to admit you're a good person. You could have easily shunned me like everyone else—and deservedly so—but instead, you showed me kindness. I won't forget that, and I was hoping that perhaps you and Anthony would consider being aunt and uncle to this little one," Lola said, rubbing her belly.

Evey was surprised and softened.

"I would love that, and I'm sure Anthony would too," Evey said, smiling softly at Lola.

Evey unlocked the door, and Lola followed her in.

"Wow! Evey, it's looking nice. Analac is amazing. Those pillows and curtains are beautiful," Lola said.

"I do love Analac. I'm glad she has you to help her," Evey said, and Lola smiled at her. "It's still a work in progress, but it's home. Anthony pulled up all the carpet and sanded the floors, stained them, and polished them. I painted a lot of walls and really cleaned everything. We still need a stove, washer, dryer, and a coffeepot!"

Lola laughed. "But it looks really good. I mean it when I say I'm happy for you."

Evey smiled at her, feeling like she had made an unexpected friend.

Chapter 20

Evey and Lola walked back to Analac's. On the way back, they passed up the men putting the tents up. Evey whooped and whistled at her grandpa and Anthony. They both laughed and blew her kisses. Anthony was surprised to see her and Lola together; but she did live with Analac, and he knew Evey didn't see her as a threat anymore.

They walked into Analac's to hear the older women laughing.

"What are you crazy ladies talking about?" Evey asked as she made her way into the sewing room.

"Oh, honey, I don't think you want to know," Grandma said, laughing hard.

"Why?" Evey asked nervously.

Never being one to hold back, Analac said, "We were just all reminiscing on our first time to spend the night alone with a boy— oh, I mean man."

She smiled her big toothless smile and nudged Evey in her ribs.

"You're right. I didn't want to know!" Evey shrieked.

"So, Pale Granddaughter. How was it?" Analac asked, wiggling her eyebrows.

"Analac!" Evey exclaimed.

"Well, we may have been born at night but not last night," Belle spoke up now, laughing too. "Why do you think we sent Lola with your clothes this morning?"

Evey looked at Lola and Lola tried to give her an encouraging smile.

"You three are so bad!" Evey said, covering her face with a leather shirt.

"Ha-ha! Well, you are to be married, and with the way you two danced with each other . . . well, your bodies know what they want," Analac said, shrugging.

"Honey, you're going to marry him. I promise to hold no judgement. I guess you're old enough to know now," Grandma was saying.

Evey looked scared at what her grandma was about to say.

"I was a month pregnant when your grandpa asked my daddy permission to marry me," Grandma continued. "Luckily no one was the wiser, and I just told them the baby came early. But I came to find out my mother and grandmother knew all along. But us women stick together."

Evey's face was red hot, and all the ladies were staring at her.

"I'm not going to give you details!" Evey shrieked again.

Lola was laughing so hard that she started tearing up.

With Grandma there, they finished up pretty quickly. The ladies kept poking fun at Evey. Lola said she was glad for her to have a turn.

"Oh," Lola exclaimed.

Everyone looked at her.

"The baby just moved," she said, face brightening up.

"Can I feel?" Evey asked.

"Well, you are the aunt, so of course!" Lola said, grabbing her hand and placing it to her stomach.

Evey waited patiently and then a little thump hit her hand, and she looked up at Lola with a bright smile. Analac and Belle were smiling. They were happy to see the two young women come together.

"Did you say aunt, Lola?" Belle asked.

"I did. Evey has agreed to be his or her aunt, and I hope Anthony will agree to be uncle," Lola said, squeezing her hand.

Belle smiled at this and explained to Grandma that it essentially meant Evey is her godmother. Grandma smiled, pleased with her granddaughter.

"You two have certainly become friends after a rocky start," said Analac.

"Yes, and I'm grateful for her forgiveness, kindness, and friendship," Lola answered. "Pale Granddaughter doesn't even have to be kind to me, and it would be understandable, but she chooses to be. And when I had everyone turn their back on me, she offered help. Anyone can plainly see she and Anthony belong together, and I was just jealous. I didn't like her for reasons that had nothing to do with her, but now I like her for who she is."

Evey had tears in her eyes, and she smiled at Lola and put a hand to her heart as the ladies all smiled.

"It's always good to have good girlfriends," Belle said, smiling at the women in the sewing room.

Next, they went back to Belle's to start making sides. She taught Evey and Grandma how to make Indian flatbread. They sang and danced in the kitchen together and made a mess as they cooked.

Anthony and Grandpa came in at lunchtime to see the crazy ladies shoulder to shoulder in the kitchen, singing at the top of their lungs and swaying their hips.

Grandpa looked at Anthony and said, "Burgers?"

Anthony nodded, and they snuck back out before being noticed and went to town. They also stopped by a few stores. Grandpa bought them a coffeepot, filters, and coffee. Anthony told him he didn't have to, but Grandpa assured him he wanted to. Anthony hugged the man and said a warm thank-you.

"Son, I'll love and treat you as if you're my own blood. My Evey chose you, so you are my grandson now," Grandpa said, squeezing his arm.

Anthony had a lump in his throat. He missed his grandfather so bad, but he was happy to have a grandpa.

"I've really missed my grandfather and feel like I'm blessed to gain another amazing one in you," Anthony replied. "To see the relationship you have with Evey makes me so happy, and I'm glad to get a piece of you too."

They both nodded at each other without needing to say anything else.

Being done with setting up tents and stacking wood, Grandpa and Anthony went back to little house on the hill to see what else they could accomplish for the day.

The men came walking into Belle's house at suppertime. There was an assortment of food, as the ladies had been cooking most of the day. Lola and Analac stayed for dinner too. It was fun to be at the full table and laugh with everyone. Evey kept looking across at Anthony.

Tomorrow, he would be chief, she thought, swelling with pride.

He noticed her staring at him, and he smiled.

They ate their dinner and walked Lola and Analac home.

On the way, Lola spoke up, "Anthony, I would like to ask you to be my child's uncle. Evey said she would be the aunt, and I was hoping you would agree too. You are a man of integrity, and seeing how you're really the only man that talks to me now, I, uh, just think your presence in his or her life would be important. And I'm sorry for everything. You deserve Evey, and I'm proud to call her my friend now. She's really my only friend. All the other girls turned their backs on me when I got pregnant and when I needed a place to stay. I've had to learn a lot of things the hard way the last months, and one thing I have learned is to surround myself with good people. Will you be the uncle please?"

Evey squeezed Anthony's arm, and he looked down at Lola with tenderness.

"It only seems right that if my bride is to be the aunt that I be the uncle," he said. "I would be honored. And for the record, I much prefer the person you are now. Being humble is a good thing."

She smiled up at him and thanked him.

Evey and Anthony walked the rest of the way home in silence, just thinking.

As they were coming upon the hill, Anthony asked her, "Are you sure you want to be the aunt and I the uncle? Lola and I have a past, and I never want you to feel weird or burdened with her. If it's too much."

She stopped him and took his face in her hands and spoke in their tongue, "Beat of my heart, I am not burdened, for you are by my side. We are bound together, and we chose each other. We cannot let our sister be without help in her time of need. We will be leading our people, and good leaders are not kings but servants."

Anthony hugged her as if he were trying to take in her very essence. She understood what it would mean after the ceremony tomorrow, and she was right, he would choose her over anyone.

Chapter 21

Evey woke up to see Anthony standing naked looking out the window of their room. His backside was to her, and she tried not to stir too much so she could take sight of him in. He seemed to be deep in thought.

"Good morning, chief," she said playfully.

He turned around to smile at her.

"You're finally awake!" he said.

"Well, forgive me for being sleepy after last night," she said, laughing. "Oh, do I smell coffee?"

"Yes you do. Your grandpa insisted on buying you a coffeepot yesterday," Anthony told her.

"God bless him!" she said, jumping out of bed and running to the kitchen, just as naked as he.

The coffee was so good. It wasn't anything special, but it was coffee in their house. She was smiling in the kitchen as she held her coffee when Anthony made his way to her.

"What are you smiling about?" he asked her.

"I'm just so happy. I can drink coffee in my house naked. I feel so free!" she said, spreading her arms out wide, careful not to spill her coffee.

Evey got dressed, kissed Anthony, and then headed out the door to go help finish minor things. She and the other ladies laid the tablecloths out, made a few more last-minute items, double-checked everything, and had a quick prayer for Anthony. The ceremony would start in the afternoon and last through the night.

She got her and Anthony's clothes from Analac's and walked back home. She was thinking about breaking the clay pot that night and announcing their marriage plans and then getting married the week before her grandparents left. There was a lot being crammed into two weeks, but she was happy nonetheless and literally had a village to help her.

She saw her grandpa's truck as she got closer to the house. He was backed in. He and Anthony were unloading something. It was a stove! Evey raced up, careful not to drag the garments.

"What are you two up to?" she asked.

"Grandma had to one up my coffeepot, and she got you a stove," Grandpa said acting upset.

Evey laughed.

"And Grandmother gave us her old washer and dryer because she's getting a new one. We are all set now," Anthony said.

Evey was so happy, and then she saw the screen door. It was a white screen door like she wanted, but it had a tree cut out of the wood for where the screen went. It was stunning.

"Oh, Anthony. The screen door—I love it!" Evey said, walking toward it.

"I figured you would. It's taken me a little longer than I thought it would, but your grandpa helped me finish it," Anthony said.

The two men got everything all hooked up, and Evey sighed blissfully. She was grateful for her grandpa and all his help. Grandpa left to go spend the day with Grandma and Belle, resting up for the long night ahead. Evey and Anthony both needed to shower and rest as well. That night was a defining moment for both of them. It would be a night sang about in their people's histories.

Evey and Anthony went inside hand and hand. They were silent for a long while, both thinking about what was to come.

Finally, Anthony broke the silence.

"So a shower then?" he asked her, wiggling his eyebrows at her.

"Beat you there!" she laughed, running down the hall to get to the bathroom.

And as she went to step in, Anthony swooped her up by the waist and kissed her neck.

"I'd say it's a tie," he told her, as she quit wiggling and softened into him and his embrace.

"Fine," she said, giggling.

They took a shower together, enjoying each other's spectacular views. Anthony thought he could never get tired of just looking at her. She was his, and tonight, everyone would know that she would be his forever.

She was rinsing her hair, and the soap bubbles ran down her breasts; and he just had to reach out and grasp them. She gasped. He smiled. She liked it when he touched her, and he liked that too. She finished washing and got out of the shower. He wasn't done yet and was a little peeved that she was leaving him alone. He had made his intentions clear. He shook his head and finished up.

Anthony walked out of the bathroom in nothing but a towel and walked to his room to get some clothes on to lounge in until it was time to get ready for the ceremony. As he stepped into his room, he stopped right in the doorway. Evey was lain out on the bed invitingly, with nothing on but her necklaces and her feathers. His breath left from his lungs, and he let his towel drop to the floor. She wanted him too. He walked slowly to the bed, with his wet hair hanging long at his shoulders. He slowly crawled his way up her length, leaving lingering kisses as he made his way up to her mouth. He gave special attention to more places than others.

By the time he made it to her mouth, she was breathing hard. She spread her legs to welcome him and wrapped them around his hard body and pulled him down to her. She knew exactly what she wanted, and it was him. He kissed her slowly and passionately. She pulled him down tighter with her legs and gasped a little when she felt him, just barely touching her most intimate area. She was ready for him.

He looked down at her, wanting to memorize her in nothing but her Indian necklaces and feathers. She was his woman—his Indian—and going to be his wife. He smiled at her, and she cocked her head to the side, trying to figure out what he was thinking. Before she could ask, he pushed his length into her; and the question and the world melted away.

They lay in bed naked and panting. Anthony asked her why she didn't let him take her in the shower.

"Anthony, I've had you by a tree, in a feed room, in a stream, on a muddy bank, on the floor, over the bathroom sink, and I just wanted you in the comfort of our bed. It's a lot easier on the knees and back, although I have a fondness for the outdoors," she said wistfully, thinking back to earlier rendezvous.

He chuckled and kissed her head. They took a nap in the comfort of each other's arms.

They both woke up some hours later, panicked, thinking they were late for the ceremony. Luckily, they weren't. But if they didn't get ready immediately, they would be.

Evey carefully got their clothes out. Anthony watched her put on the beautiful blue-and-white beaded, blond leather dress. She was breathtaking. He noted she didn't put on any undergarments and smiled to himself. Evey turned around to see him watching her, and she just smiled back at him.

"Do you want me to help you with your hair, Anthony?" she asked him.

He simply smiled at her and nodded. She carefully took the hair by his ears and braided it back. His hair would remain long that night with the wearing of his headdress. She looked him over in his leather pants and beading to match hers and was glad he would only be wearing a leather vest. He put on his leather necklace with the arrowhead that Evey had returned to him. She got the necklace she had so carefully worked on and placed it over his head and let her hand follow it to the center of his chest.

"This is really nice, Evey," he said, grabbing her hand. Lastly, she got his owl feather and put it in is hair. She stepped back to look at him like he was a masterpiece—well, to her, he was.

He kissed her mouth and took her hand and said, "Let's do this."

Chapter 22

Everyone was already at the ceremony. They were just waiting on the soon-to-be chief and his woman to show up. It was customary for him to come last and the crowd rise to show respect.

Anthony held on to Evey's hand tighter as they started seeing the tents in the distance and the big fire already set ablaze. By the time he took his sacred vow, it would be burning at full height. He and Evey were a sight. They demanded attention as they walked up. Both were so tall, elegant, and beautiful; he was dark, and she was light; but both were very Indian.

Everyone stood with their mouths agape when they saw them. They were perfectly matched in their dress. It was clear that they were together; he was so fierce and friendly at the same time, and Evey appeared so beautiful and kind. Tudley was beside Evey, wearing a matching beaded collar. The people stood in awe. They thought how she could be friend to wild beasts. There were many Indian tales of beasts and human.

Anthony nodded at a few people and made his way to the front of the crowd. He was standing in front of the grand fire, still holding Evey's hand. She stood tall and strong by his side. She would always support him and be his strength when he needed it.

"My brothers and sisters," Anthony began to speak in his tongue to his people, "I come to you tonight as your humble servant."

He squeezed her hand at this, and she hid a smile.

"As my fathers before me, I come to take my place as chief of this great people. I am honored by each of you here. I give my vow to lead you in the wise way of the old ones and protect our values and lives. With me, you will also gain a great leader in this woman who holds not only my hand but my heart."

He looked to her and smiled now and she smiled back.

"Thank you, great ones, for your faith in me, and I give my word to have faith in you," Anthony finished.

The tribe cheered in acknowledgement and agreement. Analac, the eldest among the people, then came forward, holding all his ancestors' headdresses.

"The spirits have spoken and may your sons lead after you," Analac spoke. "We put our lives and faith in your hands, great one, as you now become our chief until death."

Anthony bent his head, and she placed the headdress on his head. Evey teared up, but she wasn't the only one. Belle let out a few tears, so proud of the young man standing before them. Belle now walked up and kissed each of his cheeks and, to the crowd's astonishment, did the same to Evey.

"I pledge my allegiance and loyalty to our chief and to his chosen woman," Belle spoke up now. "As you know, Pale Granddaughter is a descendant of the first chief, and this place she could have taken, but she said she trusted Pale Daughter's choice and would stand firmly by hers. Tonight, I would like to invite her to our family. This ceremony is one for our history, as chief and his woman will bust open the clay pot that their ancestors buried so long ago to find its mysteries and forever cement our history."

Belle handed Anthony the pot.

Anthony looked at Evey, and she nodded. He placed the pot on a small table and picked up a rock and busted it. Evey's eyes filled with tears as she saw the items for the first time in something other than a vision.

"As you know, I am a seer," Evey spoke up now. "I have seen the past—our ancestors' pasts. My loyalty lies with Apovini's family, as also with Pale Daughter's. These were their most prized possessions."

She picked up Apovini's feather and held it up.

"This was the great leader Apovini's first feather. I now put it in our chief's hair," Evey spoke up now, gently touching Anthony's hair that was cascading out from under the headdress and putting the feather in. "This feather was Pale Granddaughter's that belonged to her father, the first chief. I now put it in our chief's hair as a sign of my trust in him."

She then put the feather in his hair.

Anthony reached down and grabbed the last feather and said, "This was Pale Granddaughter's feather. She had to hide it before saving our people by marrying a man she didn't love. I now put it in my chosen one's hair."

And he gently put the feather in her hair.

"This bone ring was made by Apovini, in a time where rings meant nothing to our people. But he knew it would, to Pale Daughter. He had intended on marrying her, but life had other things in store. He placed it on Pale Daughter's finger, and if only briefly, they were one."

He got down on his knee in front of Evey. Their people all took in a deep breath.

"Tonight, I ask Pale Granddaughter to let me put this ring on her finger for not a brief moment but an entire lifetime. I have loved you since we first met eyes, and the red thread that binds us is a strong one. With you by my side, I can lead our people well. I love you with every breath in me and with the fire of the sun. Will you take me as not only your chief but your husband for all time?" Anthony asked with so much love.

Evey knew they were planning on telling their people tonight of their upcoming marriage, but to see him down on one knee and him pour his heart out to her in front of everyone was almost too much. She let a single tear fall.

Evey smiled at him, took his face in her hands, and, in their people's tongue, said, "Beat of my heart, I am already yours in all but name. If you love me with the fire of the sun, then I love you with the tides of the moon. I will be yours for all time."

He took her left hand from his face and kissed her palm and then slowly slid the ring on her finger and kissed the ring. They were both smiling, and he stood up and grabbed her in his arms and kissed her. Their people erupted in jubilation!

Anthony stopped kissing her. There was one more thing left.

He went back by the table and pulled out the little rabbit skin bracelet and held it up.

"This rabbit skin bracelet was made by Apovini for Pale Daughter," he said. "I have every intention of putting it on my daughter's wrist one day. May we be blessed with a daughter one day, as bright and beautiful as you."

Then he kissed Evey on the top her head, and the crowd all let out a sigh together.

"Now let's eat!" Evey shouted, and everyone erupted in applause.

Everyone was so excited. They got a new chief and a wedding announcement all in the same ceremony. The people were also so happy that they shared breaking the clay pot with them. They knew of it but had no clue it would be opened in front of them.

Evey and Anthony got so many congratulations. Her grandma had cried seeing them vow their intentions and love to one another. Grandpa held her hand through it. They were happy to see Evey happy, and Tudley didn't care as long as people kept dropping stuff under tables for him to eat.

Lola came up to the happy couple and hugged them both.

"Lola, your dress turned out great! You look good! Glowing, as they say," Evey told her.

"I think you're the one glowing," Lola replied. "What you two said to one another . . . oh, it was wonderful."

"And how's my little niece or nephew tonight?" Anthony asked.

"Restless. The little booger keeps kicking me!" Lola said.

They all laughed.

Analac came up and gave both of them her best. She hugged them both so tight and told them she was so happy.

"It's good you're not waiting to get married," she whispered to them.

Anthony and Evey looked at her, puzzled.

"You're bound together by more than just a thread now," she said and walked off.

"What did she . . ." Evey trailed off and looked at Anthony.

"Are you—"

Anthony started to ask, but then they were interrupted by Lola's parents coming to congratulate them.

They were normal-looking people. Nothing remarkable about them at all, but they seemed like good people. Evey wanted to ask about Lola, but Anthony beat her to it.

"So did you hear Pale Granddaughter and I have agreed to be aunt and uncle to Lola's child?"

They looked up in astonishment.

"Really? Why? The child is not of our blood and is a bastard," her father said.

Evey's face went hot.

"Sir, my great ancestor was adopted by the first chief," Evey's said. "Technically, my blood is not of yours either, but love bound me to our people, and it didn't stop the first chief loving Pale Daughter. It's not an ideal situation, but a child cannot help to whom it is born. I pray your hearts soften."

They looked at her, shocked at her words, but dared not to say something negative to the chief's woman. They parted ways.

"Already making chief decisions, I see," Anthony said, nudging her.

"I really hope they can come back together for the baby's sake at the least," she replied.

God, I love her, Anthony stopped to think a while.

The night went on for a long time. There was dancing and music, of course. Evey and Anthony did their fair share of dancing. It was a hot summer night. Grandma and Grandpa were tired and went back to Belle's early to go to bed. Evey and Anthony both hugged them tight and thanked them again for everything. Lola's old friends came walking past and congratulated Anthony and just looked at Evey. Anthony gave them a hard look, and then they spoke to her.

"How special you must be, Pale Daughter, to marry the chief of our people," one of them said.

Evey smiled at them, and Anthony tensed up.

He was worried she may say something bad, so he said really quickly, "She is more special than I could ever possibly explain."

Evey put a hand on his arm. "Ladies—and I say that loosely—but, ladies, you can fight it all you want, I am one of you, even if my skin is in fact pale. My heart is here. I feel bad for you all if everything is only skin deep. When you tear someone down, you're only truly tearing yourself apart. My grandmother said that ugliness comes out in wrinkles and blemishes as you get older. I'd be careful if I were you."

Their faces went gray as Evey suppressed a laugh.

Lola then walked over. The girls stared at her protruding belly.

"Hey, girls. How are you?" she asked them.

"Looks like better than you," another said.

"I guess that depends where you're looking from," Lola said.

This confused the girls.

"I'm understanding that one real friend is better than five fake ones," she finished up.

Evey put a hand on Lola's shoulder.

"Oh, so you two are friends now? Lola, the things you said about her. Hmm, does she know? And is the baby really yours, Anthony, and you're just trying to get your girls in a row?" a girl in front said.

Lola's face went hot.

Evey spoke up here because the two on either side of her were about to blow up.

"You will indeed be an ugly old woman. How sad for you to be a vessel of such hate. I do know what Lola has said, but I choose forgiveness and friendship. Anthony cares for all his people, and you would do well to mind your tongue about your chief. If one of the elders were to hear you . . . oh my, I hate to think. As far as the baby goes, the baby is mine. I am the precious miracle's aunt. We care for everyone, especially those who cannot care for themselves. Mind that, will you?"

All their mouths dropped wide open, and Evey smiled again. The group of girls walked off.

She turned to Lola and said, "Are you okay?"

"I thought they were my friends. I was so dumb. They are right. I said awful things about you. I do not deserve your friendship," Lola said, tearing up.

"I choose who to be friends with, and I choose you. I know you are sorry. You're a good person, and you heard what I told them. That's my niece or nephew you have in there. I won't abandon him or her. Plus, you're the closest thing I've ever had to a sister," Evey said, meaning every word uttered.

Lola hugged her with the intensity of a momma bear.

"I love you, sister," Lola told her and walked off.

Anthony stared at his woman in awe. She was always surprising him in a good way. She stepped in and kept him from being ugly. She stepped in and comforted Lola. She stood by them. She stood by him. She stood up for an unborn child.

Evey looked up at him and softly touched the feathers she had placed in his hair earlier and looked at the ring on her left finger and smiled. He kissed her gently. He didn't care who saw.

"It's so loud here. You want to just go get some air and some quiet?" Anthony said.

Evey nodded. "Yes please. If only for a moment. My head is hammering."

He took her by the hand, and they walked out away from the party and into the woods, to a clearing with a big rock. Evey sighed as she saw it. She went and sat, and he sat by her.

"This is where I told you I would set your soul on fire," Anthony said, kissing her ring finger.

"It is. You have certainly done that. I'm so proud to be your wife soon," she told him.

He had one more thing to ask her.

"Evey, you do understand that once we are married, there's no turning back at all. We do not believe in divorce. The only way people split is by death. So once you officially take me as your husband, you're stuck with me forever," Anthony said.

"Anthony, I am yours forever, I am bound to you," she smiled at him. "There's no turning back for me. I can't live without you, Beat of My Heart."

He kissed her nose, both her eyes, and then her mouth. She was his. Evey had her hands on his chest, and when she moved into his lap, a leg on either side of him, he went hard, knowing that he saw her put nothing under her dress. Immediately Evey was straddling his lap. She continued to kiss him, her hair falling around them.

"Are you supposed to do any other chiefly duties tonight?" she asked. "I mean will anyone be looking for you now?"

"We have a little time," he said, smiling at her.

"All I need is a little time," Evey said, hand running down between them to grab him.

He smiled and bit her shoulder. She untied his leather pants, and he was ready for her. He had been ready since she straddled him.

"Oh, looks like you're ready for me," she said, smiling.

He smiled and grabbed her by the neck to pull her lips to his, and then he slid his hand between her thighs.

"Seems like I'm not the only one ready," he said on to her lips.

She sighed, and he bit her lip. He had his hands on her hips now and pushed her down onto him. She moaned and threw her head back and bounced on him. Even her neck was sensual to him. Her knees were hurting on the rock, but she didn't care. She came down on him hard, and her body exploded into sensation. He put his mouth on hers to cover her squeals.

Just as quickly as she was on his lap, he was shaking in conclusion with his head in between her breasts. They both started laughing looking at each other. They had already made love that day and just couldn't help but have each other again.

"Do you think we will always want each other like this?" Evey asked.

"As long as I can breathe, I will want you," Anthony said, kissing her on her chest.

They made their way back to the party. It was still going strong. No one noticed their absence with all the food and dancing.

Anthony visited among the men, and Evey went and sat with Analac and Lola.

"Are you having a good time?" Analac asked.

"Oh, yes, very much," Evey said.

Analac studied her and said, "Oh I see. You are flushed, daughter. And is that a bite mark on your shoulder?"

Evey looked down to her shoulder to see a perfect slightly pink bite mark. She looked at Analac and shrugged. There was no point in denying it. Analac laughed and gave her a shawl.

"You're the best, Analac," Evey laughed.

Lola was silently laughing too.

"I hope to be loved like you someday, Evey," Lola said.

"You will be loved in the most special way in a few months," Evey replied as she rubbed Lola's belly.

Analac smiled at both of them. "I'm proud you two girls, understanding how to grow up and forgive. Friendship is one of life's greatest gifts, and I love you both."

Both girls simultaneously hugged her.

"Analac, don't you have a birthday coming up?" Lola asked.

Analac laughed and said, "After thirty, you lose count, and they don't really matter anymore."

They finished the night laughing together and talking with other tribeswomen. They were all excited about the upcoming wedding, offering Evey advice. She smiled and graciously accepted all the advice, even if she wasn't going to use it.

Finally, Evey was too tired to even stand. She gave Anthony a look, and he nodded. She met him at the front of the great fire.

"Family, I'm so glad to have celebrated the night with you and appreciate the many congratulations and advice, but we must retire now. We look forward to celebrating our marriage with you next week. Good night, and may the moon shine bright on your dreams," Anthony said, and chief and wife walked home, hand in hand.

Chapter 23

Evey stood in front of the screen door with one of Anthony's shirts on, holding a cup of hot coffee in her hands. There was a giant red headed woodpecker methodically making his way from one tree to another. The tapping of his beak into the wood was comforting to her. Evey always felt comfort in nature.

Tudley was still sound asleep. Last night's festivities had her good boy still tired. She smiled. Their people lost their wariness of him, and the children played with him all night—that is, when he wasn't under a table eating dropped food. He had figured out sitting under children was the best place to get food. She smiled to herself.

She was so lost in her thoughts that she didn't hear Anthony come up behind her. He wrapped his arms around her waist and rested his head on top of hers. She sighed back into him.

"Look at the woodpecker," she said.

"I was wondering why you were just standing inside the screen door watching instead of sitting on your swing," he told her.

"I didn't want to scare him off. He's a beautiful bird," she said.

"He is indeed. I'm going to go get me a cup of coffee. I'm still tired myself from last night," Anthony said, walking to the kitchen.

"Do wedding parties last as long?" Evey asked him.

"They do for everyone but the bride and groom," he answered.

She looked to him, confused.

"Well, the bride and groom are not expected to stay long, as people understand they want to, um, consummate the marriage," he said, wiggling his eyebrows.

"Does consummating a marriage count if we already make love anywhere and everywhere?" Evey asked, wiggling her eyebrows back at him.

"Oh yes, it counts, and I plan on consummating with you every day," Anthony said.

Evey burst out laughing. He made her so happy.

They dressed and headed to meet up with their grandmothers, Grandpa, and Lola. Analac's birthday was the next day, and they planned on celebrating her. But there were plans to be made. They walked into Belle's house, and everyone was already sitting at the table.

"Y'all are moving a little slow today," Grandpa said.

"Yes. I'm still tired. The celebration went on long after we left too," Evey said, yawning.

"Indians sure do know how to celebrate," Grandpa said.

"The wedding should be a lot of fun!" Grandma said, her face glowing.

"Oh, it will be!" Belle said.

"But first, let's plan Analac's birthday dinner," Evey said.

"I'm going to make a Texas sheet cake because she loved it back at the house," Grandma chimed in.

"I made her a new outfit," Lola said, smiling.

"I have the dinner to be catered tomorrow, so we don't have to slave in the kitchen after the chief ceremony," Belle said.

"I made her a rocking chair, and Lola sewed a pillow for it," said Grandpa.

"I made her a new wooden chest for her leather materials, and Evey bought her some new beads," said Anthony.

"I ordered the balloons, candles, and tablecloths from the party store in town," Evey chimed in.

"And the townsfolk are all going to bring centerpieces for their family tables to represent their families," said Belle.

"It sounds like it's all under control. The men of each family said they would pitch in some money for all the food. That's the most expensive part with all our people," Anthony said.

"Analac will be so surprised!" Lola said.

"I can't wait! She deserves to be celebrated," said Evey.

"That she does. Our eldest among us is a wonderful woman," Belle added.

"Okay, so the biggest issue is, how do we decorate everything with Analac living so close to the ceremonial area?" asked Evey.

"Your grandma and I will take Analac into town for lunch and shopping. You and Lola can handle decorating and setting the food out, I'm sure," Belle said.

"Oh yes we can," said Lola.

Lola looked to all the people around at the table. She felt so at home. They felt more like family than her actual parents. She was part of something, and they valued her and trusted her to help them. She rubbed her belly. She was glad to have them and know that her baby would too. She wondered how she lived her entire life not really experiencing the love of a family, the knowing that you belong somewhere.

After breakfast, everyone scattered to take care of their tasks for the day. Grandma got busy working on the sheet cake; Lola went back to Analac's to work; and Anthony and Evey headed to town to pick up the balloons, tablecloths, and candles and planned to hide them at home.

They pulled into the party store, and Evey was excited! She loved parties. They walked into the party store and little bell on the door dinged. They walked up to the counter and let them know they were there.

The clerk, a young kid of fifteen, nodded and said, "I'll get the balloons blown right away."

He hurried off into the back.

Evey started to stroll the aisles. All the themes were so much fun—pirates, luaus, butterflies, cowboys, rainbows—and then she hit the baby shower aisle.

"Anthony," she called out.

"Yes, love?" he asked, heading toward her.

"I want to throw Lola a baby shower. I doubt anyone is going to," she said, frowning.

"I think it's proper that the aunt do it," Anthony said, smiling at her.

"I wonder if she's going to have a boy or girl?" Evey wondered out loud.

Their people didn't find out. They went to the doctor in town just to make sure everything was normal but wouldn't ask the gender, and Belle, being their healer, was also the midwife. She delivered all the babies, as long as there weren't any major issues found at the ultrasound. The most daunting thought, though, was they did it the old-fashioned way—no drugs. Belle told Evey about it and told her when the time came, she would be fine. Evey wasn't sure, and she worried for Lola.

Her mind went back to the baby shower stuff in front of her. Anthony watched in fascination as her hands gently glided from one thing to the next and then decided on woodland creatures for the theme.

"I think this will work for a boy or girl. And the raccoon is so cute on it. We will just use pale greens and yellows for the colors," she said, smiling up at him.

"Whatever you want," he told her.

"I think Belle and I can just make cupcakes instead of an expensive cake, and they'll taste better than store bought. And let's just do sandwiches, chips, and some fruits and veggies. Simple," she finished off.

The balloons and other items they—or, actually, Evey—had chosen were ready. They left with a huge nine and five gold balloons and an assortment of other colors, like turquoise, purple, and yellow. The tablecloths were the same colors as the balloons, and Evey had sparkly turquoise candles in the shapes of nine and five also.

Anthony smiled at Evey's excitement through the balloons that were cramming the cab of his truck. They got back home and put the balloons and other things in the spare room and went back to Belle's house. They both wanted to spend as much time as possible with Grandma and Grandpa before they would have to leave again. They walked in to the smell of the chocolate cake. It was wonderful.

"Mmm, it smells good in here," Anthony shouted as soon as they walked through the door.

"Good! That's what I'm going for," Grandma shouted back from the kitchen.

Anthony went to find Grandpa to see what he was working on, and Evey went to the kitchen to be with her grandmothers. They both smiled seeing her walk in.

"We got everything picked up and stashed in our spare room. The candles are sparkly and pretty. While I was in the party store, I walked through the aisles and made it to the baby shower aisle. I was thinking I should plan Lola a baby shower. I don't think anyone else will," Evey said.

"I think that would be a really nice thing for you to do, but let's make it through the wedding first," Belle said.

"Oh, of course. Lola still has about three months to go, right?" Evey asked Belle.

"Yes, daughter, that's about right," Belle answered.

"Let's wait a month after the wedding and then do it. Who do I invite though? She only has us. Her old friends were awful to her last night and really to me as well. Her parents called the child a bastard to us and didn't understand why we would support Lola. I feel awful for her," Evey said, frowning deeply.

"Leave the guest list to me," Belle said. "Although the situation is not ideal, we have several wonderful women in our people who will step up to help shower the baby."

Evey let out a relieved sigh.

"Grandma, before you leave, will you write down your chocolate cake recipe? I decided to make cupcakes for the baby shower," Evey asked.

Grandma smiled at her and said, "Of course I will. I'm so proud of you. You are really shining here among your people and turning into an amazing woman. You remind so much of your mom."

Evey embraced her grandma in a hug.

Chapter 24

The next morning was party day. Everyone woke up excited, Lola especially. She had never helped plan or be a part of a party. Analac woke up, and Lola was already in the kitchen making eggs.

"Child, you are up early," Analac said.

"I wanted to get up first and make you birthday breakfast," Lola said, smiling to the great old woman who had taken her in.

Analac smiled. They ate breakfast with small conversation.

"How does it feel to be ninety-five?" Lola asked her.

"I'm not sure. I've never been 95 before!" Analac answered.

They both laughed.

Lola grabbed a gift bag from the counter and handed it to Analac.

"What's this, child?" she asked, knowing Lola didn't have any money to be buying her a gift.

"I made you something for you birthday. I can't express my feeling of gratitude for you taking me in. If you wouldn't have . . ." Lola trailed off, tears coming to her eyes.

"Oh, child. I'm glad to have you," Analac said.

She opened her gift and was thrilled to see a leather dress with delicate beading. She pulled it out gently to see a beautiful dark brown leather, adorned with fringe and turquoise, purple, and yellow beads.

"My goodness, child, this is beautiful! You've become so good at this skill! I love it!" Analac said, truly meaning her gratitude.

"Well, put it on!" Lola shrieked with excitement.

"Child, it is too nice to just wear around the house," Analac said.

"Then it's a good thing you won't be just around the house. Belle and Dottie will be here soon to take you out today for your birthday. They wanted to surprise you with a day out on the town," Lola said.

"Will you be coming too?" Analac asked, her face lighting up.

"No. I promised Evey I would help her with some wedding stuff today. She's starting to worry, with it less than a week away."

Analac eyed her, and then there was a knock at the door.

"You better go get ready!" Lola said and went to the door to let the two ladies in.

Analac didn't leave the reservation often. She didn't feel the need to, but she was excited to spend the day with her two closest friends. They took her shopping and to the farmer's market. It happened to be the right day for it. Analac picked out some fresh fruit and some handmade candles. Her two friends wouldn't let her buy a thing. She shook her head at them.

"You only turn ninety-five once. Let us spoil you!" Dottie told her.

Analac resigned and enjoyed it. They took her out to eat Italian food at a really nice, quiet restaurant.

"The food tastes better when you know you don't have to wash the dishes afterward," Belle laughed.

The other two ladies nodded in agreement. They took their time and visited. Analac knew Dottie would be leaving after the wedding, so she enjoyed her time.

Meanwhile, back at the reservation, Lola and Evey were busy working. The tents and tables had been left out, with the wedding in less than a week. They quickly put tablecloths out and put them in a pattern from one table to the next. The colors jumped out among the normal scenery. They tied the balloons to beaded vases and set them along the tables, and the big nine and five were tied to Analac's rocking chair by the gift table.

The rest of the families started showing up with centerpieces, ranging from antlers adorned with flowers to wooden stumps with vases filled with flowers on them. One family brought candles for every table. It was looking great. Anthony and Grandpa ushered in the caterers to the food table. Luckily, the caterers set up the food table so the girls didn't have to worry about it. Mexican food was on the menu. There were pans of every enchilada, Mexican rice, refried beans, queso, salsa, chips, and plenty of salad. It smelled amazing. Evey hoped Analac would want to eat after having Italian for lunch.

The families were all piling in now. The gift table was full. She wondered what they had brought their eldest and seamstress. Five in the evening was coming up now. Analac and the ladies would be home anytime. The candles were lit, and soft music was turned on. They saw the red Malibu coming up. The whole group all stood together behind the tables so they would not mess up the view of colors and decorations set out, each table reflecting the family who sat there and loved Analac.

The three women in the car had to catch their breaths when they saw the beautiful sight coming into view.

"I knew you were all up to something!" Analac squealed with excitement.

"The girls did a good job," Grandma said.

"They sure did and look at all the people who came to honor you, Analac!" Belle said.

They pulled up to the party, and Analac's eyes filled with tears as she spotted all the people whom she loved. At the head of them were the chief and two young ladies she loved as her own.

As she opened the door and stepped out, everyone hollered, "HAPPY BIRTHDAY, ANALAC!"

She put her hands to her mouth and blew them all a kiss and hollered back, "THANK YOU!"

Evey and Lola stepped forward to grab her each by an arm and lead her to her rocking chair.

"This rocking chair is beautiful," Analac beamed.

"I'm glad you like it," Grandpa said.

"Oh, I love it and the pillow!" Analac said, touching it.

"I made that for you," Lola said, kissing her cheek.

Lola's parents squirmed in the back somewhere.

"We know you had a big lunch, so we figured we can start with your presents and then eat," Evey said.

Anthony handed her the wooden chest he had made her and it had a tree carved into the top. Analac let a tear fall as she rubbed her fingers across the tree.

"This is absolutely breathtaking," Analac said.

"Open it up," said Evey.

Analac did and found an array of different beads.

"This is too much," she said, gently touching them all.

"No it's not. You deserve it all and more. The way you have cared for us and already have a wedding dress ready and keep our secrets," Evey nudged her at this, and Analac let out a laugh.

She opened the rest of the presents from their people and was overwhelmed with joy and love.

Then they all preceded to eat. Everyone was happy and visiting. Analac was still in awe of everything and got even happier when Dottie came out holding the Texas sheet cake with a sparkly turquoise ninety-five burning bright in the middle. They all sang "Happy Birthday," and it was a loud chorus. Everyone cheered as she blew her candles out.

"Whew! I'm sure glad you just got a ninety-five because we would have started a real fire otherwise!" Analac jested.

Everyone laughed at Analac's wit. That was one thing everyone loved about her.

People came up and told her "Happy birthday," and the children ran around stealing balloons off all the tables, playing with one another. Anthony looked at Evey to see her smiling while she watched the children play.

One little girl came up to Evey and pulled on her dress. Evey turned around and smiled down at her.

"What is it, baby girl?" she asked her.

"The boys won't let me have a balloon," the girl of about four whimpered.

"Them mean boys. Come with me. I have super special balloons over here," she said as she took the little girl's hand and led her to the present table to cut off the big, gold five off Analac's chair.

She knew Analac wouldn't mind. The little girl's face lit up and she hugged Evey, and Evey laughed and hugged her back. She walked back to Anthony's side, and he was smiling.

"What are you smiling about?" she asked.

"You," he said, kissing her forehead.

She put her arms around his waist and squeezed him tight. Analac had a great time at the party. She smiled, watching everyone, and she felt so loved. She loved her family; and even if they weren't bound by blood, they were hers.

Chapter 25

The week flew by, with all the wedding planning. The day before the wedding, Belle, Analac, Grandma, and Lola came and picked Evey up. She wasn't allowed to stay with Anthony the whole day and night before the wedding. Neither one was too pleased at this. They had become used to falling asleep naked in each other's arms at night, but they went along with it. It would just be one day and night, and that would make their wedding night even better.

Evey walked out the door with Anthony hot on her heels. Before she could make it down the steps to the red car, he grabbed her by the arm and pulled her back to him, planting a long, lingering kiss on her lips.

She smiled into his lips and said, "I'll see you tomorrow."

"I'll be the one waiting for you with a smile on my face," he told her back.

Evey made it to the car, and as soon as she opened the door, the ladies inside were hooting and giving her a hard time. Anthony laughed and waved the women goodbye. He loved them all.

He had work to do to prepare for the wedding. Grandpa would be coming to spend the day and night with him. Grandpa promised a couple pizzas when he came. Grandpa knew what he needed.

Anthony ached with the longing for his grandfather and whispered to the sky, "Walk with me tomorrow, Grandfather. I miss you and love you. I know you will bless my marriage."

And at that, Grandpa was pulling up, pizza in hand. Anthony smiled. Grandpa walked up and clasped a hand on his back.

"I've got food and some movies and brought my tools in case you want to work on anything. Last night as a free man," Grandpa said as he laughed.

Anthony laughed, but in his heart, he hadn't been free for a long time.

The ladies were laughing still in the car as they made their way to town. They were going out to see a movie and then dinner.

"Shouldn't we be working on wedding stuff?" Evey asked.

"Oh we are, dear. It's important to relax the day before," Grandma said.

They watched a romance movie, and Evey found it just made her long for Anthony. Then they went to eat a burger and get a milkshake.

"There's one more stop we need to make," Lola said.

Everyone looked at her, wondering what it was.

"The nail salon!" she screamed.

All the ladies nodded. They deserved to be pampered. They pulled in and all got out. They were getting pedicures for sure. They were shocked to find Lola's mother there. She was shocked to see them too. Lola ducked her head.

"Do not put your head down, child. You are with us," Analac told her.

Belle nodded to Lola's mother and told her *hi* and gave a smile. She nodded back and looked at her daughter.

She wondered how her daughter could be with child with someone not of their people, be shamed by the rest of the tribe, yet be with the best of their people. Her ears burned red. She had tried for years to be friends with Belle and Analac. She wanted status, and now her daughter and bastard child were there.

"Hello, Mother," she said nervously, walking slowly over to her mother.

"Hello, Lola. I see you're getting along just fine without me," her mother said coldly.

"Mother, they have been kind enough to take me in in my time of need. I work for Analac and have become friends with them all. I've told them more than once that I do not deserve their kindness."

Before her mother could speak, Analac walked over and said, "Everyone deserves kindness, and we help our own when they are in need. We may not agree with everything that has happened, but we do not turn our backs on those who need us. It has been our people's way since the first chief."

Analac then took Lola by the hand and led her to be with the other ladies as they found their way to the pedi chairs.

Each women let out a sigh as they soaked their feet in the jet foot tub. They were all talking and laughing among themselves. Lola's mom just watched in envy. Evey noticed her staring.

"Why don't you come sit with us and get a pedicure too? We are all getting ready for the wedding tomorrow. The more the merrier," said Evey.

Lola's mom was shocked that she invited her. She slowly got up and made her way to the chair by Evey and sat down.

"I would like to get to know all our people, and it would be nice to get to know my best friend's mother," Evey went on.

Her mouth gaped at this.

"You are my daughter's best friend, even though you know she and Anthony dated at one time?" Lola's mother asked.

"It wasn't easy to befriend her at first, to be honest, but after we got to know each other, it was clear we were meant to be friends. I am confident in Anthony's love for me, and while they do have a history together, I have his future. Plus, I'm super excited to be an aunt. I'm an only child and thought I would never get that honor," Evey smiled at her.

Even more shock crossed her face. "You surprise me, Pale Daughter."

"How so?" Evey asked.

"For you to have grown up with no knowledge that your ancestor was one of us, and in a white person's way, it's astounding you would be so much like us," Lola's mother said.

"I am one of you. Some things are more than blood or skin deep. My grandparents raised me in the way of the land and hard work, so you'll find my values line up with the ones you grew up with," Evey said firmly to assert who she was.

Lola's mother nodded at this and sat silent for a long time. The other women were proud of Evey's responses. She was already being a great partner to the chief.

"I hope to have a heart as forgiving as yours, child," Lola's mother spoke again. "I wish you the best in your marriage to our chief. It is clear to see the happiness between the two of you. I had hoped my daughter would sit in your place at one time, but when your thread isn't bound to that person, it's not a fulfilled marriage."

It seemed she spoke from experience, and it made Evey's heart hurt.

"Thank you. He does make me so happy, and I hope I do the same for him. I understand how it feels to have what you thought would happen be ripped from you," Evey said, thinking of Danny for the first time since graduation.

Lola's mother looked shocked at this, so Evey went on.

"I have loved one other man—or, boy, I should say. I loved him but now know I wasn't in love with him. He was my first boyfriend and was there for me when my parents died when I was so young and needed a friend. We were from two totally different worlds, though, and I realized too late that I would never fit into his world or him into mine, and he hurt me badly. He did something almost unforgiveable. I'm still working on forgiving him. Nevertheless, I have Anthony, and he's a million times better. It still hurt beyond belief to have everything I had hoped and planned for taken right from under my feet."

Evey's eyes filled with tears, and she looked at Lola's mother.

"I know my situation is different than yours, but you had hopes and dreams for your daughter that I'm sure feel like are lost," Evey consoled. "I can relate to that feeling, and I hope you will work on forgiveness with me."

Lola was quietly crying at the end of the row of women. Analac rubbed her hand.

"It is well, child. She speaks the truth, and hopefully your mother will hear," Analac said quietly to her.

Lola's mom looked deep into Evey's eyes, hers filled with tears too.

"I shall try," she said.

Her eyes went wide when Evey grabbed her hand and squeezed it reassuringly.

The women all relaxed and sighed as their toenails were done. Evey got hers painted turquoise, and the other ladies followed suit.

"Are you getting married barefoot then?" Lola's mother asked.

Evey laughed and said, "Yes. I prefer not to ever have shoes on."

Lola's mom laughed. The unease was slowly disappearing. The women all visited, except for Lola. She was quiet. She had a lot on her mind with Evey and her mother talking. Evey had defended her as a sister, and she could never repay that. She loved her.

With the exception of Lola's mother, the ladies went back to Belle's for junk food and more movies. Grandma made chocolate chip cookies. All of them had cookies and milk and watched movies until the wee hours. They all fell asleep, sprawled out in the living room.

They woke the next morning all stoved up.

"Who's idea was it to fall asleep on the floor?" Evey asked.

"Definitely not my pregnant butt," Lola chimed in.

They all grunted and made their way to the kitchen to get some coffee and breakfast.

"Do chocolate chip cookies count as breakfast?" Belle asked.

"I say yes if we can eat donuts too," Grandma said.

Analac nodded and pulled the cookies out, and they had coffee and cookies for breakfast. They went over what had to be done, but really they didn't have to do too much. The tents and tables were set up. The town's men already had wood out for the fire, and like Analac's party, the families were bringing their own centerpieces for their tables. The only difference was, all the tables would be adorned with white linen tablecloths and light colors down the center and lots of candles and flowers. The ladies left Evey at Belle's, telling her to take a nap and they would be back with lunch later, as they went to help set up. They wouldn't let Evey lift a finger.

Evey did in fact take a nap, and she dreamt of Anthony. She was dreaming of waking up in a fancy bed that was bright white, with sunlight coming in, and to his face looking at her smiling as she opened her eyes. She felt immense joy and peace. Nothing else happened. It was just her waking to him smiling at her. It was a good dream, and then, she really opened her eyes to see him standing over her.

She sat up quickly.

"What are you doing here?"

"Everyone is working on getting the wedding area perfect and set up, so I easily snuck over here. A day and a night without you is too long. I just needed to gaze upon your face," he said, going to his knees to be eye level with her.

She smiled at him.

"I was just dreaming of you, of waking up next to you, and—"

He didn't let her finish, and he had his mouth on hers. He was kissing her and exploring her whole mouth with his tongue when they heard the front door open. He darted up and ran for the back door. He winked at her before running off.

"Did I just hear the door?" Analac asked as she walked in with a dress hung over her arm.

"Possibly," Evey said, laughing, knowing her face was red and her lips were swollen.

"He couldn't stay away, could he?" Analac asked, laughing.

Evey shook her head no and let out a laugh.

"I was dreaming of him and woke up to him standing over me," Evey told Analac.

Analac's eyebrows went up at this, and she asked, "Really?"

Evey nodded, wondering what the big deal was.

"Daughter, you may have more gifts than you know," Analac said to her.

Chapter 26

Analac pulled the dress out of its material sleeve, and Evey gasped. It was the most beautiful dress she had ever laid eyes on. The dress was made from white leather and had a plunging neckline. It would be in the center of her chest and its sleeves were long fringe. The dress was form fitting, and the bottom was straight with floral stamping along the bottom. There was no color on, except for the small bits of turquoise on the fringe coming off the sleeves.

"Analac, it's absolutely gorgeous," Evey said.

"I thought it would suit you. The neckline is a little revealing, but I think Anthony will like it. Another reason I decided to have such a low line is so we can see your necklaces that mean so much to you. I know you love turquoise, so it only made sense to give you hints of it on your fringe, and the dress is form fitting to show off your shape, and the floral stamp makes it a little more weddinglike and elegant," Analac explained.

"I love it!" Evey exclaimed.

"Well, let's get it on you then!" Analac exclaimed back.

They stepped into Anthony's old room, and Evey took off all her clothes. They wouldn't fit under the dress. She felt a little self-conscious undressing in front of Analac.

"Don't worry, daughter. It's nothing I haven't seen before. Plus, you won't need all those clothes later," Analac said, laughing.

Evey laughed and felt better. Analac helped her get into her dress. It had a leather corset lacing in back that Analac had to lace up. She did it tight so it would hold Evey's breasts in place, but she did have little cups in there to hold them too. Analac really thought of everything. There was a simple slit in the front that lay on top of her right leg. It barely came open as she walked. Evey looked in the mirror and smiled. She looked sensational.

Belle and Grandma came in shortly after Analac dressed her. They both gasped and told her how beautiful she was. Belle came over and started fixing her hair. She defined the curls and braided her hair back on her right side and adorned it with her feathers and two turquoise beads.

Grandma Dottie helped her do her makeup. She put a sparkly light cream on her eyes and a light pink on her lips. She didn't need much. Then Grandma pulled out her mother's pearls.

"Here's something old for you to wear," Grandma said and wrapped the pearls three times around her wrist like a bracelet.

"Here's your something borrowed," Belle said, placing a new feather from the chief's headdress in her hair.

"Here's your something new," Analac said, putting turquoise earrings in her ears to match her dress.

Evey had tears in her eyes.

"Don't you dare cry and ruin our work," Grandma said, squeezing her hand.

"I love all three of you so much! I have to be the most blessed girl alive to have three amazing grandmothers," Evey said, meaning it with every fiber of her being.

Lola came in next.

"Oh, Evey! You look so beautiful," Lola said, smiling at her friend.

"Thank you," Evey said, smiling back.

"I made you an anklet to go with your dress and earrings. Working at Analac's has its perks. I knew exactly what to use," she said, bending down to put the turquoise anklet on her ankle.

"I feel like a princess!" Evey exclaimed.

"Well, granddaughter of my heart, you are basically a queen, seeing how you will soon be the chief's wife," Belle said.

Anthony and Grandpa were getting ready too. Grandpa just put on his starched jeans and a white shirt—classic but nice. Anthony put on white leather pants that had fringe down the sides, dotted with turquoise beads here and there. They were of the highest quality. He chose no shirt for this occasion. He knew Evey liked to look upon his chest. He put his necklaces on, the one Evey made him, and his arrowhead necklace. He also put on his armband made from silver. He looked handsome yet fierce.

"Good thing it's summer, son. I have to say yours will be the first marriage I witness where the man's half naked," Grandpa said.

Anthony let out a hearty laugh. "I guess it would be. This is pretty traditional for us though."

"I'm not knocking you, son. If I looked like that, I'd probably never wear a shirt," Grandpa said, nudging him.

Anthony put on his headdress, and he and Grandpa walked out the door to head to the ceremony.

The rest of the ladies had to finish getting ready. Analac went back home to put on her ceremonial dress. As the elder, she would marry them. This made Evey so happy. Grandma wore her leather dress from the first time they were in New Mexico. Analac just added some beading to it for her to match Evey, and Belle also wore a similar dress with matching beading; the same for Lola. They would be standing beside the couple. The marriage was not only just of Evey and Anthony but for the two families as well, and they were very much part of the ceremony.

Grandma donned her red lipstick, and they were ready. Evey rubbed Lola's baby belly as if she were Buddha to get some good luck, and they slowly made their way to the grounds where Grandpa, Analac, and Anthony would be waiting for them.

Evey held no flowers. She was in between her grandmothers, arm in arm. Lola went and sat in the front row. Drums started play when Evey and the two women she loved most came into view. Anthony's eyes went up the road to try to glimpse her coming. Finally, the three women made it to the end of the aisle. Evey smiled up at Anthony. His breath was literally taken away. His bride was gorgeous in her white dress, and her neckline plunged so low without showing anything, teasing him. She was the most beautiful woman in the entire world to him. Evey smiled and only saw Anthony, and he only her.

The women made their way slowly down the aisle, and when they got to Anthony, each grandmother kissed Evey on a cheek and took the hand on their side and placed them in Anthony's answering hands. They then each kissed him on a cheek and went to stand behind Evey. Grandpa stayed behind Anthony.

Anthony smiled down at her with her smaller hands in his larger ones. Evey let her eyes search him. He had left his chest bare, and she wanted to touch him so badly. They turned to face Analac who smiled her big toothless smile at both of them.

"Sons and daughters, today is a joyous day for us as our chief takes his chosen one to be his partner for all time. This day will be marked in our histories and sang about for all time. We thank God that we may be witness to this union," Analac said, and then she chanted this song in their tongue:

> Love that binds you,
> love that sees you through,
> may you two be one forevermore,
> bountiful harvests may you store.
> We bless your marriage,
> bear many sons and daughters and keep our heritage.
> God bless the two that choose one another,
> may He be the wife's cover.
> God bless the union with your best,
> may she be her husband's rest.
> May their spirits rest in each other's embrace
> and find each other again when they leave this place.
> Love that binds you,
> love will see you through.

Evey had tears well in her eyes. This was forever.

"Now, my son and daughter. Your red thread is bright and true. Let your love guide you and you rely on each other, not the world around you. If you have words to speak to each other, now is the time," Analac said.

"Pale Granddaughter, my love and the fire of my soul," Anthony went first, "I thank God every day that he bound us together. In you,

I have found a happiness that I didn't know possible. You make me proud every day. You are not only my love, but my best friend and partner. I pledge to you all my love, the work of my hands, and my protection. I love you."

"Where the Wind Blows, beat of my heart, I love you with more than the heat of a thousand suns," Evey followed. "You have been the beat of my heart since my first time seeing here. You have literally held me up when I was at my most vulnerable. You have wiped my tears and made me laugh. You make life happy every day. You show me love every day, and I trust you completely, and I'll honor you as my husband and the head of our home. I love you."

Everyone let out a sigh.

"Our traditions do not hold much value in rings, but Evey's family does. and they would like to have the outward shown here today," Analac spoke up again. "We will honor their choice. Evey, place your ring on his finger."

Anthony held out his left hand, smiling at her. She put a silver band on his finger. On the inside, she had it engraved, "Beat of My Heart." He smiled at her, and she smiled up at him.

"Now you, chief," Analac said.

Not only did he have the bone ring, but he had another with it. It was silver with flowers stamped on it and a heart-shaped turquoise stone in the middle. It looked gorgeous next to the bone ring. He slid it on her finger and then kissed the rings on her hand. He also had his engraved, "Fire of My Soul."

"Now our bride and groom will drink from our wedding cup," Analac went on. "It is a single cup with two drinking spouts, to signify two separate people, but one life and love together."

She handed them the cup, and they took their turns drinking from their side. Then Analac went around her little table and came to them.

"You are now of one life and love. You have pledged your love together and intentions to be one. We honor you and your marriage," Analac said.

She then took her little hands and marked two streaks under each eye with blue paint. This signified they were in the same family. She then did that to everyone standing for her. Evey had Lola come up too for this, and she had Belle put the paint on Analac. This was her family.

"Now with the full support of your family, we set you on your new journey," Analac spoke with a smile. "Kiss your wife."

Anthony smiled and grabbed Evey to him. He picked her up to reach his lips and kissed her like no one was watching, but they were. There were mouths wide open when he finally came up for air. They laughed, and everyone clapped, even if a bit shocked. They went and sat at their family table, now side by side.

The people served Evey and Anthony their food. It was a true feast. Each family brought a special dish that was significant to their family. They all laughed and talked and enjoyed everyone's company. Lola's mom looked at the family table.

"My god, they consider her family. She wears their paint," she said of Lola to her husband.

"At least she's not alone. If they choose to take her and the child in, we have no say in that," he said.

After eating, it was time to dance. Evey and Anthony loved to dance together. They went out in front of the great fire so everyone could see. He ran a finger down her chest where her neckline plunged down. She giggled. The music started, and they did their lover's dance. It wasn't long ago that the lover's dance had made them burn for one another. Tonight, though, it was different for them.

He hugged her to him tight. He kissed her head and swayed with her. The music was slow, and they moved as if they were one. He spun her then and pulled her right back into him, grinding himself on her. He ran his hand down the full length of her back, and she got up on tiptoe to steal a kiss, and then he picked her up and spun her. He sat her down, and she danced around him, hand grazing his butt. He was hers. Then she came back to be in front of him, and he dipped her and planted a kiss at the very bottom of her neckline drop. He slowly raised her back up and smiled at her, and they finished their dance, tightly held in each other's arms.

Any fool could see how in love they were and how much they wanted each other. Their desire was thick in the air. The two of them went around visiting and would always gravitate back toward each other or send glances across to the other. There weren't any gifts;

they weren't necessary. The food the families brought counted as their gift. Their friendship and witness to the marriage were enough.

The night was perfect, but they were ready to sneak off alone. So they did. They went home as husband and wife.

Chapter 27

They couldn't keep their hands off of each other. They were blissfully happy.

"Mrs. Contararo, thank you for being my wife," Anthony said, placing a kiss on her hand as they made their way up their hill.

"Mr. Contararo, thank you for being my husband," she replied.

They walked up the pathway to their house. They were home, and they were husband and wife. Anthony swooped her up to carry her across the threshold. She let out a shriek as he picked her up. He opened the door, and she was kissing him, with intention. She kissed him as he carried her all the way down the hall to their room. He stopped kissing her.

She looked up at him and said, "What is it?"

"Look," he said, nodding toward their bed.

She turned her head to see he had painted her tree on the wall behind their bed, and on her branch where she had sat countless hours, there were two little barn owls. He had thought of everything.

"Oh, Anthony. It's perfect. My tree and you put our owls. This is the best wedding gift ever. I love you. Did you do all that in a day?" she asked.

"That doesn't matter now, but let's just say I was up late," he said, continuing to kiss her.

He laid her down gently on the bed, and he lay on top of her. He kissed down that sensual neckline and slid his hand in the side to grab her breast. He slid it out the side toward him so he could give it some attention. Then he did the other side. Evey had her hands in his hair, and he kissed his way back to her mouth.

"Anthony, I want you," she said.

He smiled and flipped her over and started to unlace her. He kissed her back every time he undid a spot, until he was at the bottom of her back and so close to her behind. He then flipped her back over. He wanted to look upon his wife as he made love to her. He grabbed her dress by the shoulders and pulled it down off her.

Evey sat up to be level with his leather pants. She untied his and pushed them down past his hips. She stopped to kiss the inside of his thighs, and grabbing his butt, she kissed him where he longed to be kissed; and she took her time. He didn't need readying, but he had just taken his time on her. She wanted to repay the gesture, and she loved pleasing him. He had his hands in her hair now. He stopped her, wanting to look at her again.

Anthony made her lie down, and slowly he slid himself between her legs.

"I wanted to make love to my wife under her tree, as we did the first time. I love you, Evelyn Contararo," he said as he pushed his full length inside her warmth.

They both moaned with pleasure. He wanted it to last. He took his time and reveled in each sigh, moan, and quiver she let out. He was loving her right. Then she flipped over on top of him. She wasn't near as gentle. She rode him like she was running from hell's hounds. She wanted to take him over the edge. She wanted him to say her name, and he did.

"Oh god, Evelyn, Evey. Oh."

She smiled down at him, her breast hanging in his face.

He sucked one of them real hard, and she shrieked.

"Oh, wife. What you just did there—you're going to have to do that again later," he said, smiling to her.

"I'm sure we can arrange something, husband. You have a lifetime to get as much of me as you can," Evey said with a devilish smile.

They went and showered, still glowing from their lovemaking. They washed and got out. Evey was standing in the doorway of their room, just looking at the tree her husband had painted for her.

"What do you think, love?" he asked her.

"It's the best thing I've ever seen. I can't tell you how much I love it. The owls are the best touch," she said, her eyes following the branches.

On the dresser, she noticed her four-by-six photo of her tree that her grandma had brought in a picture frame made from sticks. She walked over to it.

"Your grandpa made that while I painted," Anthony spoke as she took it all in. "Those are sticks he picked up from your tree for me."

"So you've been planning this for a while then?" she asked.

"Every single day since you came here," he said.

They went to their kitchen to get water and stepped out on the porch. They could still hear the party going on.

"I wonder how long it took for them to realize we were gone," Evey wondered out loud.

"I'm sure not long, but I doubt anyone blames us," Anthony replied, kissing his wife again.

"You know I said I couldn't tell you how much I love my tree, but maybe I can show you," she said, wiggling her eyebrows and running back toward their bedroom.

Anthony laughed and chased after her. Their night was far from over.

The next morning, Evey woke lying on her stomach as Anthony sat staring at her, smiling. She smiled back at him.

"Were you watching me sleep?" she asked him.

"Guilty. I love watching you," he said.

They were both sore from their rigors from their first night as man and wife. They were so happy. She couldn't believe the handsome Indian was hers and that she could look at his naked body whenever she wanted. He got up out of bed and kissed her forehead.

"I'm going to go get our coffee going," he said as he walked away, his bare behind shining.

Evey giggled. She got up and brushed her teeth and went to the bathroom. She threw on one of his shirts. Today, they were just going to spend the whole day at home—just the two of them, in or out of clothes. It didn't matter. They would be left alone by everyone to enjoy being husband and wife.

Evey walked into the kitchen to find Anthony in nothing but an apron, scrambling some eggs. She let out a laugh seeing him. He turned around pretending to be insulted by her laughter. He stopped what he was doing and walked over to her to give her a quick kiss. It wasn't quick though. When he went to back away, Evey grabbed him by his bare ass and pulled him to her. He let out a laugh now.

"I need sustenance," Anthony breathed out as Evey pulled the apron strings untied.

She just giggled.

"Evey," he whispered as she kissed him again and let her hands wander under the apron.

She looked at him and asked, "Do you want me to stop?"

"God no," he breathed out, and she resumed kissing him and made her way down, until she had him groaning in ecstasy.

Before she knew what had happened, he had her bent over the table, giving it to her. He finished only after he made her cry out.

Still panting for air, he asked her, "Can we please make breakfast now?"

Evey laughed, pulling his shirt back down, and said, "I'm ravenous."

"I've noticed," Anthony said with a smile on his face.

Anthony made scrambled eggs, and Evey worked on pancakes. They worked together, stealing kisses and skimming touches the whole time. They were both smiling, as if it was a permanent thing on their faces. They sat at the table they had just used earlier and ate breakfast together, sharing off one plate.

She leaned into him when she was full and said, "Thank you. For everything. This home, your love, your strength—you."

He kissed the top of her head. "I should be thanking you for choosing me. I love you, Evelyn. I'm glad you're mine."

Chapter 28

Evey and Anthony's first day as man and wife was perfect. They spent the day just enjoying each other and simple pleasures. He loved that about her. She was perfectly content, just being with him.

The next day, they had their family over for breakfast. Belle, Grandma, and Grandpa were excited to come over. Evey made French toast, bacon, and fried eggs. Her grandma was so proud of her. They ate together and enjoyed each other's company. When they finished breakfast, Evey took her grandmothers to see the tree in her room Anthony had painted for her. They both gasped when they saw it. It really was breathtaking. It looked so real; like if you touched it, you would feel rough bark under your fingers.

Evey tried to hold back her sadness as she watched her grandma and grandpa from the kitchen doorway visit with Anthony in their living room. They would be leaving the next day. She wished they could just stay. Being away from them was so hard, but their life and home was back in Texas. Evey would always have a piece of her heart there.

Her grandma met her eyes, and she gave her a knowing look. Grandma knew what Evey was feeling. Evey also noticed that Grandpa was giving Tudley some extra scratches. It would be hard for them to leave here too.

Evey felt Anthony's eyes on her. She looked to him; he had a worried look on his face too. He knew she was anxious about her grandparents leaving. He got up and made his way to her. He wrapped her in his arms and kissed the top of her head. All three grandparents smiled at them. He would always take care of her.

Dinner was great. Analac cooked for them and had them over to her house. Her home was small, so she had a picnic table fixed up in her backyard. She made pot roast with carrots and potatoes, green beans, and fresh rolls. They all sat around the table under the stars, laughing and carrying on.

"To have all of you bless me by eating from my table is one of my greatest pleasures," Analac said, looking from face to face. "Thank you for allowing me to be part of your family. I love each and every one of you so much."

"We love you too. You are family, and we are blessed to have you," Grandma told her.

Lola was smiling. She was part of a family. Analac took her in, and since then, she had never felt so secure.

"I am truly the blessed one," Lola spoke up. "To have your support and love—I have no words. I have never felt safe or like I have a real family, and I have that with all of you. This little one and I are so lucky."

"We can't wait to meet that little one!" Belle said, smiling.

"Look at us. I am the chief of our people, and my family is a mixed-up bunch. Love knows no bounds," Anthony laughed as Evey kissed his cheek.

The next morning was rough on Evey. She got up early to go have coffee with her grandparents. Anthony walked her over. She was on the verge of tears. She took a deep breath before they went into Belle's. Evey walked in and sat at the table with their grandparents. She got her coffee and sank in the chair.

They made small talk, and then it was time for them to go. Anthony helped Grandpa load up all their bags. Evey hugged Grandma fiercely.

"I'm going to miss you so much," she whispered in her ear.

"Oh, honey, I will miss you too—terribly. But you belong here. This old woman can see that. Your husband needs you by his side, and I know you two will do great things together. I love you," Grandma said.

"I love you. Call me when you get home," Evey told her.

Grandma nodded and then hugged Belle and Anthony.

Grandpa walked up to Evey then.

"Sister, I love you, and I'm happy for you. You were a beautiful bride. I'm so proud I got to see it," he said.

"I love you so much. I found a man who loves like you. Give Doe an extra treat for me when you get home," Evey told him as she squeezed him with all her might.

"I will, sister," he said, kissing her cheek.

Then they were off in their little, blue truck.

Evey let a few tears fall. Anthony and Belle were on either side of her, both their arms around her.

Grandma and Grandpa made it home safely. They noticed a lot of cars at the Bailey house as they passed by on their way home. They were probably having some big party like normal with their county's finest. Danny was being groomed to be in that elite group.

They called Evey to let her know they made it and that although they had so much fun with her and the family, they were so glad to be home. Grandpa went out and checked the mail. They had let their local mail carrier know they would be out of town so he wouldn't worry. They had a lot of mail. On top was an invitation. It was an invitation for Evey. He opened it.

The invitation was for a party that night at the Bailey's massive home. Apparently, Danny was taking a head spot in the family's rice farming business and was going to college to get a degree in business and marketing. The party was to celebrate his graduation too. It was just an extravagant show for the rest of the world.

Grandpa wondered why in the world they would invite Evey as she didn't want anything to do with them.

The Bailey woman probably sent the invite, Grandpa thought. *She would never give up trying to grow her empire. Just sad what greed would do to a person.*

He decided not to tell Evey.

The next morning was Sunday. Grandpa cooked breakfast for Grandma like normal, and they headed to church. Everyone was shocked when they only saw the two of them and no Evey. They really thought she would be coming back with them.

Danny looked like he was completely defeated. Mrs. Bailey of course had to stick her nose in their business.

"Where is Evey? Is she sick?" she boldly asked. "I was shocked she didn't come to Danny's party to congratulate him."

Grandpa looked at her, and Grandma decided to answer. To her, it was better she be rude to her than her husband.

"Well, Mrs. Bailey, Evey no longer lives with us, as she lives with her husband. She's started her own life too. It is a shame she lives in another state or I'm sure she would have loved to have seen everyone at the party so they could congratulate her on her new home and marriage."

Grandma smiled really sweetly at her. Mrs. Bailey's mouth stood wide open. She had nothing to say. Grandma and Grandpa walked off. Danny hung his head down, hoping no one saw the few tears he let fall to the ground. He had truly lost her.

Chapter 29

Evey laughed into the phone as Grandpa told her about Grandma sticking it to Mrs. Bailey at church.

"You should've seen her face, Evey. Your Grandma was magnificent, and she sounded so sweet," Grandpa was saying.

"I wish I could have seen that. I miss you already, you know?" she replied.

"I know, but at least now we both have places to vacation to," he told her.

They spoke a little longer, and then she got off the phone.

Anthony came into the living room as she hung up.

"Your grandparents?" he asked.

She nodded and told him everything Grandpa told her, and they were both laughing.

"Okay, Evey, on a serious note, we need to talk about our future. I know you want to be a veterinarian. You are an Indian and a class valedictorian. We can get you grants for college, and there's a good university forty-five minutes away with a veterinary program. I don't want you to give up your dreams. Unfortunately, I'm the chief at all times. Three hundred and sixty-five days a year, I have to be available for my people. Being chief is a full-time job. Now I will conduct all funerals, weddings, or ceremonies of any type. I have to be on top of all our government-assisted programs and community programs. I have to speak at schools and colleges.

"Luckily for me, I have a job. I am a carpenter in town. My grandfather left me his business. But your dreams are now my dreams. I want you to pursue them. Being my wife will come with a lot of work for you too. You are expected to work by my side for our people. However, I want you to be more than just the chief's wife," Anthony told her.

She smiled at him and replied, "I know how important you are to your people and that your job description doesn't exactly have vacation days, but I'm prepared to walk this journey with you, as long as you warm my bed each night. I will call the university tomorrow. I love you, and I will be a good chief's wife. I mean, I am already planning a baby shower."

He smiled at her and brought her to him to kiss her. She sighed into him.

Anthony had to go to work that day. That meant Evey would work on planning Lola's baby shower. Belle was coming over, and Analac told Lola to hold down the sewing room while she met with a client. Evey made chicken salad sandwiches and sweet tea. She told them she would fix them a light lunch.

They got to the house right at noon. Evey was happy to see them. She had sandwiches already made and cut into triangles, chips and grapes set out, and tea was on the table. The ladies came in and sat down.

"So you know I want to throw a baby shower for Lola," Evey spoke up. "I already have the theme and decorations picked out, and Grandma gave me her cupcake recipe. My biggest issue is, who do we invite? Do we invite all the women or just certain ones?"

"It sounds like you already have a good start. We invite all the tribeswomen. It's better to just include everyone, trust me on that. I will make soup and salad if you like," Belle said.

"Oh, that would be wonderful. So what's the easiest way to invite everyone without Lola finding out?" Evey asked.

"I can take invitations to our little mailroom and get them to put them in everyone's box," Analac spoke up. "So if you get the invitations made and to me, I can do that part. I will help you pay for the decorations too."

"Thank you, Analac!" Evey said. "I'm assuming everyone in the tribe knows how to buy for a baby when you don't what the gender is?"

"Oh yes," Analac chuckled. "This is our way—now, your way—of things."

"So we have decorations, food, and invitations figured out. Where should we have this?" Evey asked.

"Since it's not a big ceremony, let's just use the community center. We can go up the day before and decorate even. I think that'll be easier," Belle said.

"That sounds perfect," said Evey, feeling excited.

Ten days later, the three women were at the community center after dark to decorate. Evey had gotten all the decorations and loved them. The woodland creatures were so cute. Evey had used brown craft paper to make a tree in the corner and green construction paper for leaves. Anthony actually helped her pull it off. She smiled, looking at the tree.

She had pale yellow and green tablecloths on the tables. She alternated colors on each of the eight tables, and for centerpieces she had bought stuffed animals. She had a raccoon, fox, wolf, owl, rabbit, bear, deer, and a mouse all in diapers and holding a vase with a single white rose in it. She also bought the woodland creature tablecloths for the food table and the presents table. She also bought just a half-dozen balloons.

Belle had bought Lola a cushioned glider chair in which to feed the baby. Lola would use it for the balloons and the chair to sit in for opening presents. Analac made a dream catcher, and Anthony cut out little feathers from wood for people to sign their names on for the sign-in sheet. When they finished, the ladies turned around to look, and they were pleased.

"You did good, granddaughter of my heart," said Belle.

"Thank you. I couldn't have done it without you two," Evey said, and she hugged both of them.

The next day, Evey made her to Analac's to steal Lola.

"Hey, Lola! Let me take you out for lunch today," Evey told her.

"I've got some work to finish up for Analac," Lola replied.

"Seriously, you can break for lunch. I asked Analac anyway because I knew you wouldn't want to leave if you weren't done," Evey said.

Lola looked up and smiled. "Well, don't you know me well, now."

"Sisters usually do," Evey replied, smiling.

They were in fact more like sisters now. Neither one of them had ever had siblings or real friends, for that matter; so they did treasure each other, and Evey was so excited about the baby.

"Okay, a quick lunch then," Lola said, smiling back.

"Good. Let's go," Evey said.

Evey and Lola got in Belle's car.

"Oh. I almost forgot, I have to stop by the community center to make sure it's ready for a small party. I told Anthony I'd check," Evey said, acting her best.

"Oh, okay. No biggie," Lola replied.

They pulled in. Thank goodness most people could just walk from the reservation. There were no cars in the parking lot.

"If you don't mind, come in and help me. We can tag-team it. We can each check a bathroom and the stage and the kitchen, and it won't take as long," Evey said.

"Of course I'll help you, especially if you're buying lunch," Lola said, making Evey laugh.

They got out of the car and headed for the door. Evey pretended to unlock it and let Lola go in first.

"Surprise!" everyone boomed as Lola entered.

She jumped sky high.

"Oh my gosh! You all scared me, and oh my goodness, is this for me and the baby?" she said, smiling and getting emotional.

"Yes, it's for you and my little niece or nephew. Analac and Belle helped so much," Evey told her.

Lola turned to her and hugged her as tight as she could with her bump.

"You really didn't have to do this, but I appreciate it so much. This is the best thing anyone has ever done for me," Lola said, sniffling.

"I mean it, Lola, when I call you sister. You wore our blue paint at my wedding, and being an aunt to your baby is precious to me," Evey said, hugging her again. "Now go tell everyone hi and get yourself some food. You know it's good, Belle made it."

Lola went around and thanked everyone for coming and looked at each stuffed animal centerpiece and got herself a nice serving of food. Belle made baked potato soup and had a nice Caesar salad and a huge fruit tray. Then there were cupcakes in white liners with pale green frosting and little creature picks. They were cute and homemade. Analac took pictures of Lola throughout so she could keep the memory.

"These cupcakes are amazing," Lola said, making a delighted face.

"They are my grandma's recipe," Evey said.

"You made these?" Lola asked with a shriek.

"Yes. I did," Evey said, laughing.

"Is there anything you can't do?" she asked.

Evey just shrugged, and both of them giggled. Then it was present time. Lola let the tears fall, seeing the mound of presents for her. Twenty of the ladies from the tribe were there, and they all brought at least two gifts. It was a small community. Everyone knew about her situation. She sat in the glider with a sigh.

"The glider is from Belle," Evey said, holding a pen and a notebook, ready to write down what she got and who it was from.

"Thank you so much, Belle. I can imagine rocking my baby in here, and it's so comfy," Lola said.

She opened gifts. She got plenty of diapers, wipes, rash ointment, pacifiers, and gender-neutral onesies. Analac made her a quilt, and she made a matching mobile for the crib. It was beautiful.

"There is one more gift for the baby, and it's from his or her aunt and uncle," Evey said.

At that time, they heard someone pull in.

"Come outside and see," Evey said.

Everyone got up and followed Evey and Lola out. Anthony was outside, walking around his truck, and went and opened the tailgate. In the back was a beautiful handmade crib. Lola cried for real now.

"I asked Anthony if he would make a crib for the baby, and he said only if I helped him, so these past couple weeks, I've taken up carpentry. He did it all really, though. Look at the foot of it," Evey told her.

Lola walked over and ran her hands down the crib, and at the foot of the crib was a perfectly carved cat. Lola's Indian name was Pounces like Cat, so it was perfect. She hugged both of their necks.

"I love you both. I don't know what I'd do without you. This is the most beautiful crib. I'll treasure it forever," she said, and the guests awed.

Belle, Analac, Evey, and Anthony helped Lola get all her stuff to Analac's. Analac had turned half of her sewing room into a room for Lola and the baby. They got the crib brought in, and Lola made the tiny bed and hung the mobile Analac had made.

"It's getting real," Lola said.

"Before we know it, we will have a baby to love on," Evey said, smiling.

"You know, my mother wasn't at the shower today. I know you invited her," Lola said.

Evey looked down.

"I'm sorry, Lola. It's her loss. Maybe after the baby gets here, she'll want to come around," Evey said, rubbing her arm.

"Enough of that sad stuff. Let's get all this baby stuff organized!" Lola shouted.

Evey smiled and helped her friend get ready.

Only a month and three weeks to go until they're blessed with a new baby.

Chapter 30

Evey was so tired by the time she and Anthony got back home. She enjoyed going through all the baby stuff. She hoped to need to do that one day too. She looked up to Anthony as they dropped into their couch. He would be the best father. She took his hands and kissed them.

"What was that for, love?" he asked.

"These hands make beautiful work. I'm so proud of you. That crib was so lovely. You paint, make things, and you care for me with these hands. These hands make me feel good and wanted and can comfort me when I need it. Your hands are beautiful," she told him, still holding his hands.

He looked deep into her eyes and kissed her softly.

"These hands like to please you," he said as he slowly took his hand from hers and started to rub from her collarbone, down to her stomach, and then slowly down her waistband.

She let out a breath, and he smiled against her lips.

"That's right. Let my hands work on you," he said, and they did.

Evey woke the next morning feeling well loved and happy. Anthony was already gone. He was building cabinets in a new house in town. She went to their living room and called her grandma to tell her about the baby shower and how good the cupcakes turned out.

Then she called the university. She explained who she was and her situation, and they were happy to accommodate her. She just needed to get her high school transcript sent over to them.

She was excited. She had an amazing husband, and in a couple months, she would start college to fulfill her dream of being a veterinarian. She would be ready for it.

Evey went over to Analac's. She wanted to check in on Lola. When she got there, Lola was not there. Analac was there and was going to go out to the woods to visit with the trees.

"Pale Granddaughter, would you like to join me? You won't hear what I do, and I may not be able to share it with you, but I wouldn't mind the company. I am getting old, and walking in the woods by myself isn't always the best idea," Analac said.

"I'd love to, Analac. I love the woods," Evey said.

Analac grabbed a basket and told Evey to always take a basket into the woods.

"You never know what you might find, and there are always plants to pick to be used," the elder added.

Evey followed Analac down the little dirt path into the woods. She breathed in deep. She could feel the world lift off her shoulders as she stepped into the woods. Analac watched Evey smiling. Evey had her eyes closed, her hands held palm up, and she was just breathing and taking in the sounds.

"Pale Granddaughter, what are you listening for?" she asked.

"I'm not sure that I'm listening for anything in particular. I just feel stress leaving me, and I like to hear the wind in the leaves and the birds sing. I'm not sure," Evey said, shaking her head.

Analac studied her. "You miss your tree, don't you?"

"Silly, but yes very much. Anthony has his rock here, and I guess I was hoping to feel pulled to my own spot. My tree at home, I don't know how to explain it, but it always was a place I felt safe, and I would feel drawn to it. I guess it could be my ancestor loved that tree too. I'm not sure," Evey tried to explain.

"Things work differently than we would expect sometimes. You are in tune with life around you, and that is something special, Evey," Analac said.

Then Analac turned and started to chant her song lightly under her breath:

> Tales in trees, come talk to me. I promise to speak truth.
> Tales in trees, come set your spirit free in me.
> Tales in trees, in ancient way, your secret will stay.
> Tales in trees, I come to thee with a listening heart true.
> Tales in trees, let me see what you'd have me do.
> Tales in trees, come talk to me.

Evey found herself humming along. She knew the song from her vision when Analac let her hold her necklace. She followed behind Analac, and then all of a sudden, she stopped and tilted her head. She walked up to a great oak and pressed her hands to it and circled it, singing. Evey watched her in silent awe. Analac was smiling. When she took her hands off, she bent, moved some leaves by the base of the tree, and picked up a necklace.

"One of the kids from our people lost this necklace a while back while playing. I'll have to get it to her. She may get in trouble if her mom finds out where I found it though. Sometimes it's best to keep things to ourselves," Analac said, chuckling.

Evey wondered what the tree told her. Evey followed her some more, humming with her singing. She watched Analac do this several times and find some good plants. Evey wondered what the trees sounded like.

Is it a small, still voice in her head, or something more booming, or no sound at all? Evey thought. *Maybe it's like my visions.*

She smiled as she watched the old lady of whom she was so fond. They started on their way back home.

They turned on to the little dirt path to see Lola heading their way.

"I guess she's coming to look for us," Analac said, smiling.

"She's getting huge," Evey said, chuckling.

Lola looked up to see them coming out of the woods, and she waved. The two waved back at her, smiling. They made their way down to the path carefully.

"I heard you humming. You remember the words to the chant from your sight with me?" Analac asked.

"I do. I'm sorry. I hope that wasn't inappropriate," Evey asked sheepishly.

"Not at all, Pale Granddaughter. It did my heart well to know you remember. It's been so long since I've heard anyone even hum the tune besides me," she told her, smiling.

A loud, thunder-like clap sounded, and Evey heard something whiz past her.

Was I just shot at? she thought in a panic.

She crouched to the ground, pulling Analac with her. At that moment, they looked up the path to see Lola crumple to the ground.

"Lola!" Evey screamed as she got up to her feet to run to her.

She made it to her quickly and bent to her knees. There was blood staining Lola's shirt just under her left breast.

"GOD, NO! LOLA, LOOK AT ME!" Evey screamed at her, were shaking. "Oh god. The baby!"

Her insides cried out.

"Lola, I need you to look at me. Let me see your eyes," Evey now said, finding her calm voice.

She wouldn't help her by panicking.

Lola's eyes fluttered, and she looked up to Evey. Evey now had her head cradled in her lap and was taking her shirt off. Evey pressed her shirt down hard to Lola's wound.

I'm sorry, Lola," she cried out. "I have to try to stop the bleeding. You're going to be okay."

Analac had made it to them now.

"Oh, great spirit. Oh no," Analac breathed out.

"Analac, we need help. We have to get her to a hospital now," Evey said as calmly as possible.

"I'm going now. I know a shortcut to a house just on the other side of the trees. I'll get help," Analac said, dropping her basket and running off the path to their left.

"The baby," Lola gasped out.

"The baby will be fine. You just keep breathing. You're both going to be okay," Evey said, trying to fight back tears.

Lola was gasping now. Evey knew her lung had been hit, but her other one was okay.

You can live with one lung, right? Evey thought, seeing the pain in Lola's breathing.

"Take care of my baby. Make sure the baby knows me," Lola said.

"You're not going to die, Lola. You are going to keep breathing and help will come," Evey told her firmly. She was still holding tight on the wound and was stroking Lola's hair with her free hand.

She heard footsteps coming. Anthony was coming. He was sprinting fast towards them. His face went pale when he saw the scene. Lola was gray. Her eyes were dimming and she was gasping for air in horrible pain. Evey was placed under her, cradling her head in her lap with only her bra on. She was using her shirt to try to slow the bleeding and she was covered in blood and she was rubbing her friend's hair and gently talking to her.

"Lola after this is over, we are going to get another pedicure. Just you and me. It'll be glorious," She told her.

Lola tried to smile at her. "Evey, I'm sorry," She panted out.

"You have nothing to be sorry for Lola," Evey told her.

Lola nodded her head slowly and, with extremely shaky hands, took her bracelet off and held it toward Evey.

"Lola, I'm not taking your bracelet. You will be fine!" she said through clenched teeth.

"I want you to hold it and see. You need to know. The baby. I'm sorry. I love you, sister," Lola said in between gasps.

Evey looked dumbfounded. Lola wanted her to see something. Evey wouldn't deny her hurt friend. She nodded and stopped stroking her head and held her hand out palm up under Lola's so all she would have to do is drop it. Without hesitation, Anthony was behind her, holding her up and placing his hand on Evey's on Lola's chest to steady her and keep the pressure.

As soon as Lola's bracelet hit her palm, it felt hot and heavy. She was seeing through Lola's eyes.

Lola had a hard childhood. Her mother beat her. She beat her for spilling drinks as only a toddler. She beat her for getting blood on her carpet when she came in with a scraped knee at eight. She beat her for not keeping Anthony. She told her she must not be much of a woman if she couldn't keep the soon-to-be chief in her bed.

Evey was crying. Her best friend—her sister—was beat and belittled by her own mother. The vision continued.

She was happy. She was dating Anthony. He was sweet to her. She let him have her and really felt nothing for it. She couldn't accept him just being kind to her. She was always waiting for the something bad to happen, and she didn't treasure him. She went out with her friends and got drunk and slept with another guy, and she liked it more because he was rough with her. The way she felt she deserved to be treated.

Oh, Lola, Evey thought through her seeing.

Lola cried when Anthony broke up with her, but she really wasn't broken over it. She saw herself in Lola's eyes the first night she met her. She thought she was pretty and it was odd to see a pale face in their dress, and she envied the way Anthony looked at her. And when she saw them dance, she had a sinking feeling deep down.

She met Danny, Evey's ex, at the Indian ceremony last year. He was looking for Evey. She thought maybe she could get Anthony back, but when she saw Anthony stand to defend Evey, she knew they were finished. She had run out crying and went into town with her friends. They were hanging out at a local late-night restaurant similar to IHOP. It was four girls, Danny, and his cousin.

They looked pretty roughed up. Anthony had gotten the best of them, and Evey saw that Lola knew Evey had beat Danny too. Lola and Danny sat in silent misery together, neither one eating like the others. Danny got up to go to the bathroom, and she got up too, wanting to go get air.

When Danny came out of the bathroom, he saw her. They just came together, trying to drown out their broken hearts and crushed egos. They were making out in front of the restrooms. They made their way out to the car he and his cousin had driven in to New Mexico, and they continued kissing in a frenzy in the back seat. Neither cared if someone saw them. They wanted to not feel anything.

Evey's breath caught, and Anthony stroked her back. She continued breathing deeply and felt sick to her stomach.

Lola and Danny were in the back seat of the car, hot and heavy. They were ripping at each other's pants. What they were doing wasn't love making—this was more animalistic. He bore down on her hard, and she bit and scratched him, each enjoying the blows of the other. She was imagining Anthony's hands on her, but it was Danny who was pounding on top of her and pinching her nipples and it was Evey's name he screamed out as he poured into her.

They both looked at each other wild-eyed when they finished, not sure what just happened or what to say. They had had sex all right. But they weren't banging each other; it was the other in their minds.

Two months later, she was puking in the bathroom. She thought she just had a stomach bug, but one of her friends teased her and asked her if she was pregnant. She quickly told her no but then had a horrible feeling deep down. She bought a test that night, and it came out positive.

She thought about getting an abortion, but she didn't have the money to. She went to her purse and found on a crumpled napkin Danny's phone number. He had written it down to not seem like a complete jerk after they used each other. Lola felt sick. She had made a baby out of anger and hurt, not love. She didn't even really know the guy, and he had cried out for Evey.

She dialed the number and a woman answered.

Evey felt sick. She knew that voice—Mrs. Bailey.

"Hello Bailey residence."

"Um, hi. My name is Lola. I'm looking for Danny. May I speak with him?" Lola asked.

"He's not here at the moment. Would you like me to tell him you called?" Mrs. Bailey asked.

"No, I don't think so. I uh. I can call back," Lola stammered.

"Are you okay, dear? You do not sound well. How does Danny know you?" Mrs. Bailey asked.

"We met at the reservation. I'm okay. I just need to speak with him as soon as he has a chance," Lola said.

"This is his mother. What is so urgent? What's going on? You can tell me. I'm very close with my son, and he tells me everything. So whatever it is, dear, he'll tell me anyway," Mrs. Bailey said, sounding sincere.

"Mrs. Bailey, I . . . there's no good way to say this. I'm pregnant with his child," Lola said quickly.

"Are you sure?" Mrs. Bailey asked.

"I'm sure," Lola said, sobbing now.

"Okay, we can fix this. I'm going to send you a bus ticket, and you will come see me and Danny, okay?" Mrs. Bailey instructed her.

Lola gave her the information and, three days later, was on a bus to Texas. She was in awe when she saw the huge house. She was nervous about seeing Danny. The second time you see someone shouldn't be to discuss a baby. To Lola, she was relieved it looked like the Baileys had plenty of money to help her care for the baby.

She knocked on the door. Mrs. Bailey opened and stepped outside. She looked taken aback when she realized Lola was Indian. She didn't even let her in the home.

"Hi. Is Danny here too? I'd really like to talk to him," Lola said.

"No, I'm afraid not, dear. He's working on some college stuff. So I've thought about your situation. I'm going to write you a check for twenty-five thousand dollars, and that will be more than enough to get you an abortion and for you to do something with. We really don't want any babies over here. It's just not the right time in Danny's life, and, well, we don't mix," Mrs. Bailey said with arrogance.

"So Danny doesn't want the baby?" Lola asked.

"No, dear. He's not ready, and by the looks of you, you aren't either. Here, take this check and go back to the bus station and go back home. We never have to talk about this again. Actually, don't ever call or come here again," Mrs. Bailey said, and she turned and walked in the house and left Lola standing outside with a check in her hand.

Lola did leave. She felt lower than a stray dog. She couldn't believe how cold the woman was, and she thought her mother was bad.

On the way back home, she saw a billboard that had a baby on it, and it said, "All life is precious, no matter your circumstance." That was her sign. She was keeping the baby. She had craved to be loved so long. Now she would have someone to love her.

Evey dropped the bracelet and had tears falling down on Lola. Her eyes looked glazed even more now, and her face was twisted in pain. This made Evey cry more.

"I'm sorry, Evey," Lola gasped out. "Now you know. Take care of my baby. Check is in bottom of my purse. I'm sorry."

Evey cradled her more tightly to her.

"Quit apologizing to me. You don't need to. I love you, sister. You don't have to apologize. I'm sorry for what you've endured on your own. You are so strong, and you are a good person. You chose your baby's life. And you chose my friendship over harboring jealousy and rage. I love you. Hang on. Help will be here soon."

Anthony wasn't sure what Evey had seen, but he could tell it rattled her. He was rattled too by all the blood and the gurgling sound coming from Lola. She was drowning. Then they heard sirens. The ambulance couldn't make it back on the trail, but they saw Analac leading the paramedics and the stretcher.

The paramedics assessed the situation quickly. It looked like something straight from a horror film. A young half-naked girl cradling another girl with both of them crying. She didn't want to let her go.

"We have to do our job, ma'am. We will do our best," they were telling Evey as they pried Lola out of her arms.

Evey was in a daze. She followed as they loaded her friend who was fighting for every breath into the ambulance.

"We will be right behind you, Lola. You are not alone," Evey spoke firmly.

She looked to Anthony who was already getting Belle's car. They would all be going together.

Chapter 31

Anthony floored it as they followed the ambulance. Belle had grabbed Evey just one of Anthony's white shirts that was at her house still. Belle sat in the front, and Analac held Evey, who was sobbing in the back seat.

"You did so well with her, granddaughter. Let's pray for her and the baby now. That's the best thing we can do," Analac said, comforting Evey.

They made it to the hospital right behind the ambulance. Evey and Anthony ran out, chasing the stretcher.

"She needs to go back to the OR right away," said the paramedic as they ran in.

Lola looked Evey in the eye now and said barely audibly, "If you have to choose between us, the baby."

"I promise," Evey whispered, blinking back tears.

Lola weakly nodded at her and mouthed, "I love you."

"I love you. Now go fight," Evey choked out.

They turned a corner, and Anthony and Evey were stopped by hospital staff.

"I'm sorry, you can't go any further. The waiting room is just that way on the left," a woman in scrubs said, pointing down a hall.

Evey couldn't hold herself up anymore. She fell into Anthony, and he picked her up and carried her to the waiting room. He sat her in his lap and cradled her like a baby, and she had her head deep in the crook of his neck, sniffling. Belle and Analac made it to the waiting room, also tear streaked.

They sat down on a couch and held hands and prayed together. The rhythmic sounds of their chanting soothed Evey as Anthony rocked her. He stroked her back. He watched the hell she endured as she cradled her bleeding friend. He saw the defeat in her eyes when she promised Lola she would make the impossible choice if she had to. He prayed she wouldn't have to. He also felt a deep pride for how she cared for Lola. She didn't falter. She had ripped her shirt off and took care of her without a second thought.

Then a doctor in blue scrubs with weird blue slippers and a blue hat came in the waiting room.

"Are you Lola's family?" he asked.

"We are the closest she has," Belle spoke up.

"But you're not blood relatives?" he asked.

"My name is Chief Anthony Contararo. I am the leader of my people. I am considered blood relative to any of mine," Anthony spoke up.

The doctor nodded. He was familiar with the American Indian culture as this was the closest hospital to the reservation.

"Lola has lost a significant amount of blood. The bullet went through," the doctor spoke. "How I do not know, but her lung is badly damaged, and some major vessels were hit. I need to know her wishes. I don't think I can save her and the baby, with the amount of blood she lost and her trouble breathing. The baby's heartbeat is already strained. With her breathing, she's not getting enough oxygen for herself, let alone the child. Do you know what she would want?"

Evey stiffened and stood up.

"I promised her we would save the baby. She said if it was between her and the baby"—Evey took a deep, shaky breath—"save the baby, and if you can, please save her. But that was her last wish."

Anthony stood beside her and nodded at the doctor.

The doctor put a hand on Evey and said, "I promise you I will do my best."

He turned and walked out, and Evey let out a scream. She was filled with so much frustration, anger, and sadness.

As if Anthony knew what she was thinking, he said, "The police are already out there looking for evidence. We will find who did this. Thank god they only shot once."

"Once was all it took. They hit her, and the bullet whizzed past me too. I heard it," Evey said, tears falling again.

Anthony got the worst look on his face and pulled her to him so tight. "You are safe now, and they will do their best with Lola. Shhh, now. It'll be okay."

But he knew he was lying. It wouldn't be okay. Being chief was about to get real. He looked over to his grandmother; and she, with her knowing eyes, bowed her head.

It felt like an eternity that they sat in that waiting room, all just praying. Evey really didn't have a clue how long they had been sitting there when she saw a group of nurses rush past with a little space shuttle on wheels. Evey jumped to her feet. She just knew that was the baby. She had to go. She ran down the hall, chasing them.

One of the nurses turned around to see Evey chasing them.

"Is that Lola's baby?" she hollered.

"Yes, but we have to get her to NICU now," the nurse said. "She needs help breathing."

She. She. She, was all Evey heard in her head. *I have a niece!*

She dropped to her knees in the hall and cried and prayed to save her sister and to save the baby girl. Anthony came and found her. He dropped to his knees beside her.

"C'mon, love. Come back to the waiting room. We have to wait to hear news on Lola. The doctor hasn't come back yet. Did they say anything about the baby?" he asked, looking so worried. "Had the baby died?"

"They were rushing her to the NICU. I think that's baby ICU. She needs help breathing. She's a girl," Evey cried into his shoulder.

He helped his wife up, and they supported each other as they walked the hallway back to the waiting room.

"Did the doctor come back in yet?" Anthony asked his grandmother as they walked back in.

Belle just shook her head no.

"The baby is a girl. She needs help breathing is what one of the nurses said," Evey told the two worried faces.

"She will be fine," Analac said. "She is tough. Babies are resilient."

They heard footsteps coming their way. The doctor walked back in. He didn't need to say a word. His sad face said it all.

"No. No. She's gone," Evey busted out crying

The doctor grabbed her hands and nodded.

"We worked on her for over an hour, trying to bring her back," he spoke gently and matter-of-factly. "Her body just couldn't handle it all. She fought long enough for her daughter to be brought into the world. She is premature and was struggling beforehand due to her mother's injury, so she's in the neonatal intensive care unit. Her breathing isn't quite right, but the doctors and nurses there are the very best. I know this is so much to take in, but decisions need to be made. Who is her next of kin?"

"I am. And I will be caring for the child. I am her aunt. Can I go to her?" Evey spoke up and asked, not wavering.

"I will have a nurse come and get you as soon as the child is stable. We will have someone else coming to speak with you shortly on where we go from here."

Evey looked up confused at the doctor.

"My son is the chief, and he will preside over the funeral," Belle spoke up here through her tears. "You may send her to NM's Family Funeral Home, and we will handle it from there. Thank you for trying hard, Doctor."

He nodded and looked down sad and took off down the hall toward the NICU.

Evey was in a daze. She just planned a baby shower for her best friend, a woman whom she considered her sister. How could she be planning her funeral?

Evey, Belle, Analac, and Anthony all crowded together on one couch and cried and cried. It wasn't just that they lost someone they loved; it was how she went. It was ugly, and it was painful, and it was done on purpose.

All of a sudden, Evey looked up.

"What is it?" Anthony asked.

"Her bracelet. I left her bracelet on the ground," Evey cried.

"We will go get it, love. Do you want to tell me what you saw? I know Lola was upset about it, and so were you," Anthony said.

Belle and Analac looked at Evey at that comment.

"Lola handed me her bracelet in those last moments outside," Evey started to speak. "She couldn't really talk at that point. She wanted me to know the whole truth about the baby. I got more than that though. Her mother beat her."

She choked back sobs, and a horrible pain in her stomach shook her.

"Lola never really knew love until she became part of our family. She really loved us and was looking forward to being a part of our family for the long run. Going back to the baby, the second night that Anthony and I danced the lovers' dance, my ex, Danny, showed up. You remember?" Evey asked.

Everyone nodded.

"After the all-out brawl, he and his cousin and Lola and her friends went out to eat. Lola and Danny were both in a bad place after seeing that Anthony and I were meant for each other, and they had sex in the parking lot in a car. I will spare you the gory details, but Lola regretted that the baby was made out of anger and hurt and not love. That's how she got pregnant.

"She found out at two months and called Danny's house to tell him. His mother answered the phone and pried the information out of her and told her she would help her. But her help wasn't really help. She bought a bus ticket for Lola, and Lola showed up at her home in hopes of getting help and talking to Danny. But Danny wasn't there, and Mrs. Bailey told her they didn't need the baby. She told her to go get an abortion and wrote her a check for twenty-five thousand dollars to shut her up. Lola couldn't do the abortion, needless to say, but she still has the check in her purse. She told me. She wanted me to know for the baby. I wonder if I should call Danny and tell him he has a daughter," Evey finished up.

"No," Anthony said firmly.

Evey looked at him with question in her eyes.

"If he didn't want her, it's none of his business now," he answered.

A nurse walked in and said, "Are you Lola's family?"

Everyone doubted she really needed to ask, judging by their disheveled looks and puffy eyes. They nodded.

"We have the baby girl stable. She has to be on oxygen, and we have her in a special bed to keep her warm until her body can regulate temperature on its own. It's normal for preemie babies not to be able to control their body temperature. We just need to keep a very close eye on her. The first twenty-four hours are critical."

"Can we see her?" Evey asked.

The nurse looked her and looked her up and down and grimaced. Evey looked down. She was filthy and covered in blood.

She cried silently, shoulders shaking.

"I just need to see her. I won't touch anything. She's the last promise I made to her mom, my sister," Evey said quietly.

The nurse nodded with a sad understanding. "Come with me."

Anthony walked with her. They followed the nurse behind two big automatic doors. There was a sink on the other side. It had a note that said, "Everyone must wash hands before entering."

The nurse paused and nodded to the sink. They turned on the water and got soap. Evey panicked as she scrubbed. She had dried blood all over her. She scrubbed and cried. Finally she stopped when her hands felt raw.

The nurse handed each of them a yellow coat to cover them.

"I'm sorry, but don't touch anything. This is a very delicate area. I'll lead you right to her," the nurse said.

They followed her in to a tiny space bubble. Evey gasped when she saw the tiny, little baby girl. She had oxygen on her nose and an IV going into her foot. But she was still beautiful. She had the tan skin of the people, but her hair was more like a blonde peach fuzz. She had Lola's mouth, and her hands were so tiny. Evey grabbed Anthony as it hit her—they were now responsible for this tiny person.

The ride back home was solemn. Evey had cried herself out, as had the others. She was still filthy and covered in her dead sister's blood. Anthony called the police station when they got home to see what they found. They asked if they could come by to speak with his wife in the morning.

"Tell them they can meet me at the hospital when I go to check on the baby," Evey spoke up.

He did, and they agreed.

Anthony let Evey take her shower alone. He had enjoyed sneaking in with her, but tonight, he knew she would need her water hot enough to make her feel like she was burning off the bad.

She just stood under the hot water for a long time, numb. She watched the red water swirl down the drain. She was stained with so much blood. She scrubbed her body and then scrubbed it again. She just didn't have a clue who would want to kill Lola, let alone a pregnant woman. Evey stayed in there for a long time.

When she got out, her fingers were pruned, and she had red skin. Anthony looked at her.

"I'm going to go shower now, love. Do you need anything?" he asked her.

She shook her head and tried to give him a smile, but it wouldn't come. He went into the bathroom and got in the shower and wept. He wept for his wife, he wept for Lola—a girl he couldn't stand for a long while—and he wept for his niece or, now, his daughter. He wept because he didn't know how he would handle the fact that the precious baby girl was Danny's.

Could I really raise his blood? Evey's ex? Anthony ruminated.

It made him feel sick, and then he did throw up. He realized he would have to be the one to do Lola's funeral. He was the chief. It was his responsibility to facilitate the funeral.

Evey was shaking. She was grieved to her core. She picked up the phone and dialed her grandparents. Her grandma answered the phone.

"Evey?" Grandma asked, and Evey started to cry again. "Hush, honey. I know, I know. Belle called me. She said you were as great as you could have been. I love you. Hush now. It'll be okay."

Evey nodded and then felt silly. Her grandma couldn't see her through the phone.

"The baby is a girl. I have a daughter now. It's crazy. I should just be her aunt and just spoil her. Anthony and I have only been married for a month, and now we have a child to care and worry about. Did Belle tell you she's Danny's child?" Evey asked.

"She mentioned it. You will be a great caretaker for that child. I know it's not ideal, but she was placed in your life for a reason. Look at how you and Anthony were brought up or Pale Daughter, for that fact. You will be okay. It takes time, you know from experience, as do the rest of us. I love you, honey," Grandma told her.

"I love you too. It never gets easier to lose someone. Do you think I should call Danny? Anthony said no, and I don't want to go against him, but I can't help but wonder if he even knows," Evey asked her grandma.

"You should talk about it with Anthony again in the morning, if you still feel like you should then. Everyone deserves to know if they have a child," Grandma answered.

"Did Belle tell you that Mrs. Bailey wrote Lola a check and just threw her out?" Evey asked.

"Yes, she told me. I wish I could say I'm surprised. She's a cold woman. Even if Danny knows, his mother won't let him ruin their reputation," Grandma said.

"You're right. I'll sleep on it. Danny really does feel sorry about what he did. I'm still not in a good place with him, but to think he has a child he doesn't know about still doesn't sit well with me. I thought he really couldn't hurt me again, and yet here I am," Evey said.

She and Grandma spoke for a long time. Evey cried more than once and was grateful for the woman on the other end of the line for being there for her to talk through what she was feeling. She hung up eventually and sagged into the couch.

Anthony walked into the living room to see his wife balled up on herself, with her head between her knees.

"Evey," he said, walking toward her.

She looked up and reached out for him. She just needed him to hold her. He went right to her side and scooped her up toward his chest. They didn't say anything and just held each other. They were too tired from crying, talking, and thinking. They just needed to be touched and held. They just need the assurance of each other's arms.

Chapter 32

Evey woke the next morning on the couch feeling like she had been hit by an eighteen-wheeler. Her whole body ached. She looked and couldn't find Anthony, but she could smell bleach. She walked to the bathroom. He had bleached the tub and gotten rid of her bloody clothes. He was a good man. She heard Anthony come in, and she turned to see him, looking awful too. He gave her a weak smile.

"Thank you," she said, closing the distance between them.

She needed to be in her husband's arms again. He held her tight to him.

"I love you," she told him.

"I love you too," he said back, planting a kiss on her lips and rubbing her back. "Are you ready to get this day going? It's going to be a rough one."

She nodded slowly.

Anthony took Evey to the hospital. The cops were there to ask her about what happened the day before. Evey's hands trembled as she relived the horrible moments of the previous day. They asked her if she saw anything. She hadn't—and it upset her she didn't—but she didn't expect to witness a murder. She hadn't seen anything out of the ordinary. She did tell them she heard the bullet whiz past her and where she was standing. If they could find the bullet, they might be able to link it to a gun.

They spoke with Anthony too because he was the chief and his input mattered. They shook both of their hands and gave them their condolences and told them they would be in touch.

After the cops left, Evey and Anthony made their way to the NICU. There was a tiny girl who needed them. A nurse greeted them with a smile.

"The baby girl is a strong one. She is still on oxygen and needs help breathing. We inserted a feeding tube to help her get stronger. You will see that in her nose. Don't be worried. It's fairly normal for us to have to do this," the nurse said as she walked with them to the little space shuttle.

Evey took a peek at the tan baby with blonde fuzz.

"How are you, baby girl? Your mommy would have loved to see you. You are beautiful just like her. Stay strong and keep fighting. You have people who love you," Evey softly spoke to the baby.

"When will we be able to hold her?" Evey asked the nurse as Anthony bent to take a good look at the baby and speak softly to her.

"Hopefully in a few days. She just needs to get her little body lined out. We will call you if anything changes and when she is ready for that," the nurse told her.

Anthony and Evey stayed for a long time just looking at the tiny thing. Evey's heart broke for the loss of her friend and the mother that child would never have. Anthony studied Evey's face.

"Are you okay, love?" he asked her.

"I'm not sure. I'm just trying to take it all in, I guess. We are responsible for her now. We don't even have a name for her," Evey answered.

"We will figure all that out. It'll be okay. We have to get to the funeral home now," he told her.

Evey closed her eyes tight. She didn't want to go there. It was like she would be accepting it then.

When they got to the funeral home, Belle and Analac were there. Analac had made Lola a burial dress, and she wanted to see it got put on her. The men of the tribe made her a pine coffin, and Anthony had carved flowers on it for her. The funeral was going to be a long one. The wake would last four days, and since Lola's parents were out of the picture, it fell on them. They had to decide where to take her, and someone had to be with her at all times, and they were expected to feed everyone.

Belle said not to worry about the food, that the tribe would come together to help on that. Anthony was going to have to perform the burial ceremony. Evey's heart hurt for him. One of his first major things as chief was a funeral. Analac said to bring Lola home to her house. That's where she was living, so it seemed right.

They got everything lined out, and the hearse would bring Lola to Analac's house that evening. Belle called some other ladies to help ready things.

Anthony had called Lola's parents the night before to tell them that Lola had passed and the baby was born, but they seemed so distant. Evey figured they were in shock, thinking they had all the time in the world to make things right with their daughter. Anthony and Analac went back to the reservation to prepare the wake.

Belle and Evey went back to the hospital to go see the baby one more time that day. Belle took a deep breath when she saw the baby girl hooked up to so many machines. She sang to her and prayed over her. She hugged Evey as she cried softly, looking at her.

"She's just so tiny and helpless." Evey whimpered.

Evey and Belle went over to Analac's. They had a special table set up in the living room for Lola. She would face toward the door so her spirit could see the sun. It was a nice sentiment. Evey's pale side was having a hard time dealing with the idea that Lola's lifeless body would be in Analac's living room for four days.

While she was at Analac's, Anthony came running in.

"Evey, the hospital called. We've got to get there now. The baby is struggling," he said, panting and in shock.

All four of them hurried to Belle's car and Anthony floored it to the hospital.

They ran down the hallways to be stopped by doctors and nurses in the hallway outside of the NICU.

"Before you go in there, we need to explain to you what's going on," the doctor said.

Evey nodded and Anthony said, "Tell us."

"The baby went into cardiac arrest. She coded, but we brought her back. She's on life support. It looks scary to see. We won't know much for twenty-four hours. She's got to decide if she wants to fight or not," the doctor said.

"I was just here earlier, and she had the feeding tube and it seemed as though she was going to be okay," Evey remarked, confused.

"Well, preemies have a mind of their own. You never know what will happen, and the baby was born in a very traumatic situation. She may have not had adequate oxygen or her organs may be damaged. We really have to run more tests to be sure. Please go in and speak to her and pray for her. We promise to do our best," the doctor explained.

"I promised her mother I would choose the baby over her. We can't lose the baby too. That was her final wish," Evey cried.

The doctor rubbed her arm. "We won't give up on her, and we will do everything we can."

The four of them walked carefully into the NICU in their yellow scrubs. Evey gasped, even though the doctor told them what to expect. She let tears hit the floor seeing the tiny girl hooked up to a machine to keep her alive. There were IVs and tubes and wires, and Evey could barely see her.

Analac wrapped her arms around Evey, and then Belle did the same. Anthony stood solid behind her. Evey was so glad to have them there because she wasn't sure if her legs would hold her up.

"Baby girl, are you trying to give me gray hair already? I'm too young for that. Use those lungs, sweetheart. I need you to figure out how to breathe and do it. I love you," Evey softly spoke to the little baby.

Analac spoke to her in their tongue, "Great-granddaughter of my heart, you will grow up to be wise, and you will live a full life. My word I give to you, and my life I will trade for you. You are loved."

Belle turned and looked at Analac as if she had said something awful.

"Analac, mo. You can't," Belle said.

Evey didn't understand.

"I've decided. I'm ninety-five. I'll talk to the Great Spirit tonight, and this child will live," Analac said with serenity and certainty.

Evey didn't understand. She looked between the women. She felt Anthony put his face down in her hair and felt him sob.

The ride back home was quiet—too quiet.

"I don't understand what's going on," Evey finally broke the silence. "Can someone please tell me?"

Analac was sitting in the back seat with her, and she took her hand, smiling.

"Granddaughter of my heart, I am going to petition to the Great Spirit tonight to take my life instead of the baby's."

"What? No, you can't do that. I don't understand," Evey said with a lump in her throat and tears in her eyes.

"Granddaughter, life demands a price sometimes, and it's a life for a life. I would much rather the child live. I have had a full life, and to go out as a sacrifice so one may live is something I'm proud to do," Analac said, locking eyes with Evey.

"Was Lola's life being taken not enough?" Evey cried angrily.

"My granddaughter, Lola's life wasn't given willingly, and there's another life that will be held for hers," Analac said.

"I hate all of this. I lost my best friend. Her baby is on life support, and you're talking about leaving me too! I can't handle that! I've lost too many I love! I can't lose you too! I love you!" Evey was screaming now, face red with hurt and anger.

Analac smiled sweetly at her.

"I love you more than you will ever know," Analac said. "No amount of time would ever be enough, my child, but that baby needs something done now. Be at the great fire in one hour. We will have all the elders present."

Evey was in shock as she and Anthony walked into their home.

"Evey, we have to get in our Indian dress," Anthony softly said to her.

"I'm not going. I'm not going to let Analac kill herself. I can't watch that. Seeing Lola was enough," Evey said through angry, clenched teeth.

"She's not killing herself. The Great Spirit may not accept her offering. But for you to not show would be the worst mistake of your life. Analac needs you to be there for her, and you are my wife. I need you there. Do you not think this doesn't hurt me? Analac has been in my life for my entire life. I'm dying inside. But some choices are not ours to make," Anthony said passionately.

"Oh, Anthony. I'm so sorry. I'm so selfish. I've just been thinking about how I feel, and I'm a horrible wife," she cried into him.

"You're not a horrible wife. We are all hurting. I need you to be strong, and Analac needs you to be strong. There's much more to our people than you know still," he said.

Evey nodded, dried her face, and got dressed.

Anthony and Evey walked hand in hand toward the great fire. They were really just holding each other up. Even grief stricken, he was still a sight in his full headdress and leathers. Evey wore her light tan dress that she wore for his becoming chief.

Analac was in her burial dress. She smiled at them as they walked up. Evey had to steady herself not to cry. Everyone, Belle included, was sitting around the fire like they did when Evey had her first seeing experience with them. Anthony sat at the head of the group with Evey on his right and Belle on his left. Analac chose to sit by Evey. She could have sit anywhere, and that's where she chose.

"My brothers and sisters, we are gathered here tonight for Analac," Anthony spoke up. "She wishes to petition to the Great Spirit on the behalf of our newest daughter who is very ill in the hospital. Analac says she will offer her life for the child's."

There were silent, sad nods all around.

Analac addressed everyone now, "My brothers and sisters, please do not feel stricken for me. I willingly choose this, and I am an old woman who has lived a long, full, happy life and wish to see this child have the same. I love you all and hold no fear of death. I know what awaits me, and I understand the choice before me."

Evey looked at her. She was so strong. She drew strength from her. Evey squeezed her hand and nodded her head in a silent prayer.

One of the elder men threw a handful of something onto the fire, and it came to life, bursting in brilliant colors. The group began to chant. Analac closed her eyes. Evey wasn't sure if she should close her eyes too, but she was mesmerized at the sight around her. She looked at Analac. She was chanting something different under her breath, and she was almost smiling. Analac looked up to see Evey watching her in awe.

Analac grabbed both her hands and put her head on hers. Evey leaned into her.

"Granddaughter of my heart," she spoke to her in their tongue, "I feel your pain as if it were mine. Please let your heart lose some of its ache. I will be fine, and so will you. I've heard so. You may not be blood of my blood, but we are the same. Our hearts beat as one, and we are linked. You saw my life, and you heard the words to the song. My gift I pass to you. Pale Granddaughter, you will be a great woman among our people, our seer and, from this moment on, the speaker to the trees. You have my blessing and the Great Spirit's blessing. I am proud of you and know you will use your gift wisely. You are my only choice. You are my chosen one. Sing with me, granddaughter."

And she did.

> Tales in trees, come talk to me. I promise to speak truth.
> Tales in trees, come set your spirit free in me.
> Tales in trees, in ancient way your secret will stay.
> Tales in trees, I come to thee with a listening heart true.
> Tales in trees, let me see what you'd have me do.
> Tales in trees, come talk to me."

"Yes, child. You are ready," Analac smiled.

She took her old shell-and-bead necklace off and placed it around Evey's neck.

Evey let a tear fall on to Analac's hand as she held the necklace around her granddaughter's neck. It wasn't too long ago she held the necklace in the palm of her hand to see Analac's life story. She looked with such love and adoration down at the old woman.

"The babe will live. You call on the trees for good, and you call on my spirit when you need me," Analac said peacefully.

Then it was quiet. Analac smiled and watched the sun rise as she let out her last breath. It was the most peaceful thing Evey had ever seen—a perfect death, so to speak, or maybe a perfect rebirth. Because as Analac breathed out the last time, a woodpecker landed on the closest tree and beat out a song.

Evey just sat there, holding Analac, watching the bird, and told her, "I see you and I hear you. Your spirit lives within me."

Anthony slowly got up and spoke, "Let the histories and songs say that Analac, Talks with Trees, gave her life willingly so that a child may live and she passed her gift on to Pale Granddaughter."

He looked right at Evey with so much love and heartache that she could have just flopped on Analac in her lap and gone with her.

Belle and Anthony walked over to Evey and bent down with her and held on to Analac in her lap with her. Her legs had fallen asleep, but she didn't care. Evey felt like she was dreaming as the men came and took Analac to her house to be laid in a coffin. She and Lola would have mourned together.

Evey didn't change from her Indian dress. She made Anthony rush her to the hospital. She knew the baby would be better. They ran down the hall to the NICU as the doctor was coming out. He was completely shocked to see them in full Indian dress and there at the exact moment he was about to call them.

"I was about to call you. It's a miracle. The baby girl is just fine. All her tests are normal, and she is breathing on her own. We are about to try to feed her with a bottle. We really have no explanation as to what happened. It's a miracle. The baby girl will be fine," he said.

Evey smiled, with tears in her eyes, and said, "Her name is Ana. The baby's name is Ana."

Anthony gripped her arms tight, and the doctor smiled.

"That's a nice name," Anthony said.

Chapter 33

Evey got to feed Ana her first bottle and got to hold her. They didn't have a camera to take any pictures, but it just so happened another mom was there and had a camera and offered to take a picture of them with their baby for the first time. It hit Evey—Ana was theirs. She thought how fitting it was that their first picture together would be of them with her in full Indian dress.

She laughed for the first time in a long time. Anthony looked at her and wanted to know what she was laughing about.

"Our first picture with her, we are in full dress. It's just so fitting. I feel like Analac had it all planned," Evey said, as Anthony kissed her.

They made it back to the reservation completely drained. They hadn't slept for a long time. They had ridden the night out with Analac and then gone straight to the hospital. Now, they headed straight for Analac's. That's where Belle would be. It was hard to walk in and see two pine boxes side by side, with two women they loved so much in them.

They told Belle how well the baby was, and then Anthony said, "Grandmother, her name is Ana."

Belle lost it. She clung to both Evey and Anthony and let it all go. She had been strong for so long, but now she let it out. Analac had been Belle's longtime companion. It would be hard for her without Analac.

"That's so perfect. Ana. We have an Ana. You two will be wonderful parents. It's kind of a shock to be parents so soon, but I have all the faith in the world in you both," Belle said.

Anthony was so scared, but Evey didn't bat any eye holding tiny Ana in her arms and feeding her. She would be fine, but Anthony was worried. His grandmother was right. They hadn't even been married long and now had a baby, and on top of all that, the baby was the product of their ex's. It didn't get more messed up than that.

They went home to rest for a little while. They were both exhausted. They showered together, just not wanting to be alone, and then they went to bed and lay down and just slept.

Evey woke up a few hours later to Anthony caressing her slowly. She rolled to her back to look at him. He had been crying. She kissed his cheeks where the tears had streamed down and looked at him. He bent and kissed her mouth and caressed his way lower. He just need to touch her, to love her, to feel the comfort of her warmth.

She opened for him and pulled his face to hers. He made slow, soulful love to her. He looked at her as if memorizing her every feature. He kissed her gently, and she rubbed his back as he finished inside her. He didn't move off her. She just held him, and he wrapped his arms around her. They needed the security of each other.

They went back to Analac's. Belle was still there. She wouldn't leave unless someone else was there to sit with them. Someone in the family was to be by their loved one's side at all times until they were buried.

Evey went and sat down and told Belle to go rest. She nodded at Anthony to walk with her, and he nodded back and took his grandmother's arm. Evey watched them walk out and sighed deeply. Oddly, she didn't feel weird sitting in the living room with two dead women. She loved them both, and she found comfort that Lola wasn't alone. She even found herself talking to them.

"Analac, I never understood what a beautiful death was until I held you as you went watching the sun come up. I named the baby Ana. I know you would like that, and I know Lola would like that too, with the way you took her in. I'm not sure on a middle name yet," she found herself saying to her loved ones.

Then there was a knock on the door. It was Lola's parents. They looked like they hadn't slept in days. Evey let them come in.

"Come in," she said and just moved aside.

She wasn't sure what to say to them. They had shunned Lola, and her mother didn't even come to the baby shower. Evey then felt a pang of grief for her friend. She died with not ever resolving the issues with her parents.

Lola's mother started crying, and her father rubbed her back. She gently touched her cheek and then looked up to Evey.

"I heard you were with her," she whispered.

Evey got a lump in her throat, but she managed to respond, "I was."

"Thank you for being there for her and not leaving her," Lola's father said.

Evey straightened up at this and said, "She was my sister. I would never turn my back on my family, no matter how awful the situation is."

She let her anger get the best of her and immediately felt bad.

"I'm so sorry. I shouldn't have said that. I—"

"It's okay. It's the truth. I have a lot of regret with the grief," Lola's father said.

Evey just nodded. She imagined he did. Lola's mother stayed quiet.

"I'm still sorry I said it. I just truly loved Lola. The baby survived. Her name is Ana," Evey said.

Lola's mother looked at her then and smiled.

"A girl. I'm glad she made it. You and Anthony will be bringing her home?" Lola's mother asked.

"Hopefully in a week. The doctors say it's a miracle, but we know the truth of it. Analac's last wish was to save her. Anthony and I have a lot to do to get ready for her, but we will raise her as she's our own. I promised Lola. Lola's last words to me were that if it was a choice between her and the baby, I should choose the baby. I will honor her wish and raise Ana to know our people's ways and to remember her mother," Evey said.

"Lola picked well to have you and Anthony as the aunt and uncle. I would like to see her when you bring her home, if that's okay," Lola's mom said.

"That will be fine. She has Lola's mouth. She really is perfect," Evey said.

After an awkward few more minutes, they left.

Anthony came back to sit with Evey while Belle rested.

"I've got everything in order for the burial ceremony. I don't know how I'm going to get through it," Anthony said.

"We will get through it together. You can fall apart on me after it's over," Evey told him, holding his face.

He kissed her cheek. She told him about Lola's parents coming by and how she freaked out and then felt bad. He squeezed her and told her she did fine.

"So we are parents now, huh?" Anthony asked Evey.

"Yep. We are, aren't we? It's a lot to take in. But I will honor Lola and do my best with Ana. I was hoping to get pregnant soon, and Lola and I raise our kids together. My, how things have changed. I was prepared to be an aunt and spoil her, but I hope I'm a good mom to her," Evey said.

"You will be great, and we will do this together like you told me. It's not ideal, but hey, we will make it work," Anthony said, feeling scared to death.

"I guess we need to get the baby stuff to our house. I'm sure glad I threw that baby shower now," she told him.

"Evey, I need to ask you something," Anthony said, and she looked at him.

"Do you still feel like you need to call Danny? If you do, I won't hold you back. I know you're my wife, I just get all animalistic with him around and feel so protective of you. I'd be lying if I told you I hadn't thought about him being Ana's father," Anthony explained to Evey.

"I would like to call him, but I'll wait until everything is settled here and we get Ana home. I feel like I should tell him she's alive, at least. His mother sent Lola to have an abortion. I know you hate talking about Danny, but he's not one to run away from a child or be okay with abortion. I just know that. Maybe I'm wrong. I hope not though.

"And it is a little weird that Danny is the father to Lola's baby, but that baby is innocent in all this. To be honest, it hurts pretty badly that they did that to us. But it's done. Hell, look at us. We weren't raised by our parents, and my ancestor sure wasn't. We will be fine," Evey said, trying to look confident, but she was also terrified.

Belle came back a few hours later with some pizzas. Evey didn't want to eat with Lola and Analac just lying in there. She just kept looking at their faces.

At least they look peaceful, Evey pondered.

"Evey, Analac passed her gift to you. That is truly an honor," Belle broke the silence. "She loved and trusted you so much. Only worthy women can have gifts passed to them, and you, my dear, have two. I'm proud to call you ours."

Evey smiled with tears in her eyes and went and hugged Belle.

Anthony was shaking as he got ready for the burial ceremony. He hated this part of being chief, and it was even worse; it was for two people he loved.

Evey walked in the bathroom to see him shaking as he went to dip his fingers in the blue paint to go under his eyes. She went and grabbed his hands to stop him, and she dipped her fingers in the paint and swiped two blue streaks under each eye and did hers. Their family unit would do that. Grandma and Grandpa mourned with them. They couldn't make it, but they did send beautiful flowers.

Evey and Anthony walked to the burial ground together. It was just on the edge of the reservation. The graves were already dug and the caskets nailed shut. He walked to the front of the crowd. Evey and Belle stood behind him on either side. The whole tribe was present and teary eyed. They did wails and Indian cries for lives lost. Anthony raised his hands up, and they went silent.

"My brothers and sisters, sons and daughters. I come to you today not only sad but in great hope. Our sisters have passed from this world to live with the spirits. Their spirits are free and travel among the winds in trees, on the wings of birds, and in the stillness of our hearts. They touched many lives here.

"Analac was our eldest and loved by everyone. Talks with Trees will be greatly missed, not only for her skills as a seamstress but as a friend and wise woman. Lola, Pounces like Cat, will be missed. Her life was cut off too short, but a piece of her lives on in her daughter. Her death will not go unpunished. The wrath of the Great Spirit will find whoever is responsible.

"I find peace in knowing that her last wish was honored and that she is not alone in her journey as a spirit. It is Analac who will help guide her, and it is Analac who gave her life to the Great Spirit so the child would live. Now, we return those we love to the ground, that they may find rest. Great Spirit, please accept our sisters and call them your own."

Anthony dipped one finger in black paint and ran it diagonally across his face and then did the same to Evey and then Belle. This was an outward show of their grief. The two caskets were lowered in the ground by a group of men, and then they sang a song with the beating of the drums.

Evey went and threw the first handful of dirt on each one and let her tears fall in with it. After they covered the graves in dirt, Belle went and sprinkled wildflower seeds over each one, and Anthony watered them in with a watering can.

"Out of death comes life, and with life comes love," Belle said.

Chapter 34

Evelyn and Anthony were running around the house, making sure they had everything ready. They would be bringing baby Ana home tomorrow. It had been a week since the funeral, and they were still just making it day to day. But they had so much to live for, Ana being part of that.

Anthony had brought the crib over from Analac's, and since Evey had helped Lola put everything up, she knew where it all was, and they got it moved smoothly to their house. They put the glider in the living room and left the wooden rocking chair in the bedroom.

Evey bought a cute little pink lamp with turquoise accents for the top of the dresser. She also bought big letters that spelled "Ana" and painted them pink to hang up above the dresser and brought a fuzzy turquoise rug for the floor. The painted mural on the wall didn't clash too bad with the girly colors. The hospital was sending home some formula. It was the same stuff Evey and Anthony were using, but they would need more.

"I think we are ready as we can be," Anthony said, taking a deep breath.

"I think so," Evey agreed, and she kissed him.

"This is our last night together as just us. Maybe we should . . ." Anthony trailed off.

Evey laughed, spanked him, and ran to their room.

Evey woke the next morning way earlier than she needed to. She was anxious about getting Ana home. She went to the kitchen to make her coffee and heard knocking. She went to the front door and opened it and looked out her screen door. She could just barely see the redheaded woodpecker.

"Good morning to you too. Are you the bird to bring Analac's spirit to me on your wings? You were there when she left," she said out loud, and somehow she knew. She smiled.

Anthony was up not too long after her, and he had his coffee and was ready to go.

"Is it time yet?" he asked.

"You heard the doctor. He won't be there until eight thirty, and it's only six now. But we can leave whenever you're ready," she said, kissing his cheek.

They wouldn't be able to wait much longer. They went out to the truck to put the car seat in. Anthony may have cussed by the time they got it secured. Evey laughed. They were running early, but they were ready to get Ana.

They made it to the hospital and parked. Anthony turned off the truck and took a deep breath.

"You ready?" ye asked.

"As ready as I'll ever be. Life as we know it is different now," Evey replied.

They smiled at each other.

Evey was still mourning the loss of her friend, and her heart ached that the baby would be going home with her instead of Lola. But she was happy at the same time. She was having a hard time with her emotions.

They walked into the NICU. Anthony still hadn't had a chance to hold Ana with all the getting ready for the funeral. Evey had come by herself a lot to see the baby and feed her at noon. Evey had already gotten to bond with her. Anthony had been worried about raising Danny's daughter.

They were early, so the nurse sent them in to sit with Ana. Evey went to her and grabbed her out of her little hospital bed right away.

"Hi, my Ana. How are you this morning? You get to come home today!" she told her, holding her swaddled in her arms.

Anthony looked at his wife with a passion he didn't know was in him. Seeing her hold a baby stirred something in him, and he loved her even more.

Evey looked up to him and smiled.

"She's so pretty, isn't she?" Evey asked.

"Yeah. She is," Anthony said, but he wasn't looking at the baby.

"Here, you hold her," Evey said, moving the bundle.

"It's okay. She's fine with you," he said.

"Put your arms out. You need to get used to one another," Evey said, not giving him an option.

Anthony put his arms out. Evey sat Lola in his arms. Any worry Anthony had about raising Danny's daughter disappeared as he held Ana and looked at her precious face. Evey smiled as she saw him melt, and she felt a stirring in herself as she watched the big man she loved so much cradle a tiny little girl.

They got Ana home with no problems, besides Anthony driving like a grandpa. He was extra careful with their precious cargo. Belle was waiting at home for them when they pulled in. They weren't going to have any visitors the first couple days so they could settle into their new life and routines. Anthony carried the big baby carrier in, and Belle was waiting.

As soon as he sat the carrier down, Belle was unstrapping Ana. Anthony went and put his arm around Evey. They smiled as Belle baby talked to Ana and rocked her.

"She's a pretty baby. Did the doctor say anything we need to know?" Belle asked.

"No. He said she is fine and completely healthy now," Evey told her.

Ana let out a cry.

"I bet she's hungry. Let me fix her a bottle," Evey said.

Anthony followed her so he could learn how. He wouldn't have his wife doing everything. He would help. He would be a good father.

◆

The next few days were a whirlwind. Both of them were trying to navigate life as parents when they didn't have months to prepare like they had imagined they would. They were both exhausted.

Ana didn't sleep all through the night. She was up every few hours to eat. Anthony was a huge help to Ana. He would get up with her to make bottles while Evey went to soothe Ana. He really just liked seeing her in his old room, rocking Ana. Seeing her hold a child in her arms made his heart all but burst.

Evey would be holding Ana so gently and patting her little bottom and sing to her, and no matter what time it was, Evey would be smiling as she sang to her. Anthony rubbed Evey's shoulders as she fed Ana. When Ana got up to lay her back down, Anthony followed her to the crib he had made and put his arms around both of them.

He spoke in their tongue, "Great Spirit, thank you for my family. Help me to protect and lead in the way that is right. I know not your ways, but I will take this gift and do my best."

Evey had tears in her eyes after she heard Anthony's prayer. Losing two women they loved and gaining a little girl to raise was hard on them both. They were both just barely holding each other together. But Ana kept them going.

Evey laid Ana down, and she had to have her husband. She turned in his arms to face him. She grabbed his face, and he had tears in his eyes. They spoke without speaking. Evey understood what he was feeling.

She kissed him slowly, softly, deliberately. He squeezed her tighter in his arms and lifted her off the floor. She picked her legs up and wrapped them around his waist, never unlocking their lips. Anthony carried his wife to their bed and lay down with her gently. He caressed every inch of her and she him.

They spoke with their bodies, arching into each other and brushing hands in only places they knew on each other. When Anthony finally came to her, the sensation was an explosion. Neither one moved; they just stayed as they were, breathing and letting their hearts beat for the other.

◆

The next morning, Anthony had to go down to the police station. This would be Evey's first day alone with Ana. He was going to find out what kind of progress they'd made, if any, in finding Lola's murderer. Anthony's shoulders looked heavy, and Evey's heart hurt for him. Being chief was a tough job.

She kissed him at the door and told him, "You are not facing any of this alone. I am with you, and I will help you carry the burden. I love you."

"I love you too," he said, standing up to his full height and put his warrior face on.

He was ready to face whatever it was headed his way.

Evey watched him pull out, and then Ana started to cry. She quickly fixed her a bottle and went to grab her. She went outside to the swing on the porch and sat down and started to sing as she fed her. The redheaded woodpecker flew overhead and landed in a tree and started to peck.

Evey smiled and told Ana, "You're great-grandmother wishes you well. Her spirit visits us."

She kissed her little head for Analac. Evey noticed movement coming up the path. It was Lola's parents. She stiffened a little. She always had a worry in the back of her mind that someone would try to take Ana away. They couldn't though; Lola had it written and clear that if anything happened to her, Evey and Anthony were to be Ana's legal guardians.

But what about Danny? He has rights, and he should know he has a daughter, right? she wondered.

Her heart hurt. Evey watched Lola's parents approach.

"Hi, Pale Granddaughter. I hope it's okay that we have come. We were told you wanted a few days to settle. We respected that. We just wanted to see her," Lola's mother said.

Evey nodded and said, "It's okay. I'm glad you came. Come look at Ana."

They both walked up to the swing and looked down. Ana was still eating. When she finished, Evey popped the bottle out of her mouth and put Ana to her shoulder to burp her. After she burped, she gently handed Ana to Lola's mother. Her mother looked shocked.

"Are you sure?" she asked Evey.

"Hold her. She may be able to give you some comfort. I get comfort from her, knowing that a piece of Lola is still here," Evey said, nodding with tears in her eyes.

Lola's father bent down and hugged Evey. Evey was surprised. The man never said much, much less hugged anyone.

Evey patted his back as he cried on her shoulder. Ana started crying, and Lola's mother couldn't comfort her. She handed her back to Evey, and Ana immediately contented and went to sleep in Evey's arms.

"She feels safe with you," Lola's mother said.

"I'm glad of it. I really do love her as my own," Evey said.

Lola's father spoke, "We can see that. Ana is in the best possible hands. Love her and care for her and do better than we did with Lola. We will see you soon. I should like to know if Ana ever needs anything."

Then he grabbed Lola's mother's arm, and they walked off.

Evey watched them leave, and she looked down at the bundle in her arms.

"I will always love and protect you, my daughter," she said.

Evey had just made an important decision. She would call Danny. She just had a pang in her stomach, and she knew she just needed to call him. She prayed it was the right decision.

Fathers have some rights, but according to law, Ana is American Indian and she would be raised by her people, Evey debated with herself. *But Danny is a Bailey, and money isn't an issue.*

Evey's stomach turned. She needed to call him.

Evey toted Ana in after rocking her to sleep in the swing. She went and laid her down in her crib and went to her living room to pick up her phone. She dialed Danny's number.

"Hello," Danny said in his deep voice.

"Hi, Danny," Evey said.

"Evey! How are you? Are you okay? I mean, I'm surprised you called," he spurted out.

Evey took a deep breath and asked him, "Danny, are you alone?"

"Yes. I am," he answered, hoping that she was okay.

"Danny, I have something to ask you, and I need you to be honest with me," she told him.

"Okay, ask me anything, Evey. I promise I won't lie to you about anything. I'm still learning to live with what I've done to you," he said back to her.

"God, this is terrible. I don't even know what to do besides ask, so here it goes. Did you know Lola was pregnant?" Evey asked.

"What? I'm confused here, Evey," he replied.

"Lola, she's the girl you slept with from the reservation after . . . you know. She was my best friend, so I know," Evey explained to him.

"Whoa, do you mean to tell me she's carrying my child?" Danny asked, sounding shaky.

"It's really complicated. She was. The baby is here. Her name is Ana. Lola was shot and died, but the baby lived. Anthony and I have her. Well, we're her . . . godparents is the easiest way to explain it, so she's been home with us. You mean to tell me you really didn't know?" Evey asked.

"So I have a daughter?" Danny asked, in shock.

"Yes you do, and she has blonde fuzz on her head. She's so pretty. But you really had no clue?" Evey asked again.

"She has blonde hair like me? I really didn't know. I feel shocked and a little sick," he said honestly.

"Lola called and told your mother, and your mother invited her down and wrote her a check for twenty-five thousand dollars for her to get an abortion. But Lola couldn't do it, and she just assumed you didn't want to be in the baby's life," Evey told him.

"So my mother told her I didn't want the baby then I guess," Danny said, putting the pieces together.

"That's basically it. She told Lola you were in college and it wasn't the right time for a baby. I couldn't decide if I should call you or not. I've thought about it for days now. Ana is a child of our people, and there are laws. But you are also her biological father, and I couldn't live with myself if I didn't tell you," Evey said, starting to tremble.

"When did you find out I was her father, Evey?" he asked.

"Lola showed me as she was dying. She didn't want to die and no one know. She had kept it to herself. She was afraid of hurting me, and she was under the impression that you didn't want her either.

Danny, I think you should come see her. Ana. She is part you, and I think you should come see her," Evey said, starting to cry.

"Are you crying, Evey?" Danny asked, feeling concerned for a woman he still loved.

"I was trying not to. I've lost two people I love, and I loved Lola as a sister, and she trusted me to care for Ana, and I guess I'm terrified you will take her away or at least try to. I don't know. That's so selfish of me, and I'm sorry. I'm so sorry," Evey said, breaking apart.

"Don't cry and don't be sorry. I know you, Evey, and I know you love that baby if you are caring for her. I would like to meet her. I won't take her from you. If my mother did all that, I can't imagine bringing a child home to that meanness, and I cannot care for a baby on my own. But if you'll allow it, I'd like to see her," Danny said, trying to soothe Evey.

"Yes. Come see your daughter and know who she is. I would be glad to know that you didn't turn your back on her. When will you come?" she asked.

"I'll be there this weekend. I'll get a hotel," he said.

"No. You can stay in our spare room and be close to Ana with us," she told him.

"I'm not sure Anthony will be okay with that. I know I wouldn't want me close to you if I were him," Danny said.

"I can understand that, but this isn't about me, you, or Anthony. It's about this precious baby girl, and I am Anthony's wife, and he knows that I am bound to him," Evey said.

"Okay then. I'll see you Friday evening. I'll have to leave Sunday though. I am in school. Don't tell anyone I'm coming. I don't need my mother to hear," he said.

"You have my word. I'll see you Friday," Evey said.

Anthony made it back home, and Evey was cooking dinner, holding a baby in her arm. He smiled seeing them as he walked in. Evey had music playing and was swaying as she stirred spaghetti sauce. Anthony walked over to her and kissed her hello, washed his hands, and took Ana from her.

Evey smiled at him and said, "Haven't you become quite the daddy."

He smiled at her and replied, "She is mine. Any worries that I had have melted away, and seeing you love and care for her and cook me dinner . . . God, Evey, I love you," he said.

She smiled at him and blew him a kiss. She finished dinner up and made them plates. Anthony went and laid Ana down in her crib. They ate in silence for a while. They both had news to tell.

"Anthony, Danny is coming Friday. I called him. He had no clue Lola was even pregnant. He wants to see Ana," Evey said.

Anthony stiffened and asked, "Does he want to take Ana? I'm not sure if I can be okay with that."

"No, he doesn't. He knows he's not in a place to raise a child, but I'm happy, I guess, that he didn't just turn his back on her. And one other thing . . . I told him to stay in our guest room. He'll be leaving Sunday," Evey said quickly.

Anthony shot squinted eyes at her. He wasn't happy at all.

"Evelyn Contararo, do you remember what happened the last time he was here? I do not like or trust him. I'm not okay with that. I don't want him here," he barked out.

"This will be the first time he sees his biological daughter, and he is going to leave her here with us. The least we can do is give him a place to stay," she said calmly.

"A place to stay? A place to stay! Ha! We owe him nothing! He slept with Lola and never even called her. He's tried to get you back. Now, I have to worry about him around my daughter and you," he said, raising his voice and turning red.

Evey started to cry.

"Evey," Anthony whispered, his face immediately softening.

She shook her head no.

She cleared her voice, and then said, "I love you, and I am your wife. *Your wife*! But I couldn't live with myself if I didn't tell him, and one day we will have to tell Ana. But you just called her your daughter. She's mine too. Do you not think I didn't feel sick calling him? I didn't want to, but I had to. Wouldn't you want to know if you had a child out there?"

Anthony looked at her and then just nodded.

"I will make it work for you and for Ana, but I won't like it," he said firmly.

"I never asked you to like it. I just know this is right," Evey responded.

"Might as well tell you about my bad news now while we are all upset," Anthony said.

Evey took a deep breath. He had been at the police station all day. She looked him in the eye and nodded.

"They have no leads as to who shot Lola and couldn't find the bullet. They checked the woods and found nothing. They are going to shelf the case," he sighed.

"How can they do that? She was killed! That's such bullshit!" Evey said with her jaw set.

"I said as much to them, but there's nothing else I can do. I've put the whole reservation on high alert, and they are to come straight to me if they hear anything, and I will personally go search for the bullet myself," he said, feeling resigned.

Evey got up and said, "I'm going to take a shower while Ana is asleep."

She didn't offer for Anthony to join her. She just went, and he sat at the table with his head in his hands.

Chapter 35

Anthony sat at the table for a while, just thinking about everything. He was a newlywed with a newborn, and there was a murder in his reservation, and he was just barely the new chief. He was saddened and worried. He was worried for his wife and his newly adopted daughter.

How could I be okay with Ana's biological father coming, especially when said father still loves my wife? Anthony racked his brain. *To top it all off, the police are zero help in finding Lola's murderer. How could I tell my people that they would just have to live with an unsolved murder on their territory?*

His life was a mess, but he still had his wife and daughter. He felt warm thinking about them, and then he felt bad.

Am I too hard on Evey? he wondered.

He let out a long sigh and got up from the table. He peeked in on Ana, and she was still sleeping. Alone time with his wife was a luxury now. He carefully opened the bathroom door. He could tell the water was boiling hot. The mirrors were steamed up. He took his clothes off and opened the curtain to look in on Evey. She was standing under the water with her head down.

Anthony slipped in and cursed under his breath as the boiling-hot water hit his skin, but he didn't stop. He put his arms around Evey and pulled her to him. He held her tight and just breathed her in. He was sorry for being short with her and sorry for the situation they were in. She didn't choose this either.

He slid his wedding band off his finger and grabbed Evelyn's hand. She looked to see what he was handing her, shocked.

"Hold it and see my heart for you," Anthony whispered.

She opened her hand, and he gently placed his ring in her palm.

The ring went heavy in her hand, and then Evey was seeing through Anthony's eyes.

She saw herself on their wedding day, and her heart filled with joy and pride. She heard him talking to the men of the tribe about how he was so blessed and that she completed him. She saw herself as he was on top of her. She saw Anthony building the crib, and she heard him doting on her and watching her in moments that she didn't know he had seen. She felt and saw the love he had for her and knew that there was nothing in the world that would make him not love her.

At last, she saw herself holding Ana in the rocking chair, and she felt such a different feeling that she couldn't describe—an overflowing love and adoration.

She grabbed the ring with two fingers from her other hand and turned around to face her husband, and she grasped his hand and slid his ring back on him. She had tears in her eyes, and he did too.

"Thank you for letting me see. I love you so much, Anthony. It's okay. We are going to be okay, and my whole heart will always be yours," she told him, looking deep into his eyes.

Anthony kissed her in way that took her breath away, and then he kissed down her body and gave every inch of her attention. He kissed his way back to her mouth, and then he had her in the shower. It wasn't just lovemaking—it was affirmation that she was his.

They dried off, smiling at each other. They were fine. They would make it through this together.

The week went by, and then Friday came around.

Anthony picked Danny up from the bus stop after finishing up a cabinet job. He was sweaty and dirty and had on a white wifebeater and blue jeans. His strong, muscular arms showed brilliantly. Danny got off the bus and looked around. He was surprised to see Anthony by himself.

Well, this should be great, Danny thought.

He walked over to Anthony and threw his bag in the back of the truck. He noticed the wood and tools in the back. He got in. They hadn't said a word to each other.

Finally, Danny broke the silence.

"Thank you for letting me come."

"I didn't let you. That was all Evey. Truthfully, I wasn't happy about it," Anthony said.

"I don't blame you. But I'm still glad, and I appreciate knowing the truth. I really didn't know. My mother is a piece of work. I was sorry to hear about Lola too. I can't believe it all," Danny said.

"It's a real big mess, to say the least. Look, I don't want to be a jerk to you the whole time, and I'm going to do my best for Evey's sake, but don't try anything and be easy with Ana. We love her. Everything is still real raw for Evey and for me too," Anthony told him, looking straight ahead.

"You have my word. I can imagine how hard it is for both of you," Danny said, looking out the window. "So the wood and the tools?"

"I'm a carpenter and took over my grandfather's business when he passed. Being chief is great, but it doesn't necessarily pay the bills," Anthony said.

Danny was surprised to hear him talk about family business.

They made it to the house, and Danny thought the little house was nice. He could see Evey in it with the white porch door with a tree and the swing. He grabbed his bag and followed Anthony in. The house smelled good. Evey had a chicken in the oven.

"Where's Evey?" Danny asked.

"She's probably rocking Ana in her room. Be quiet, in case she's asleep," Anthony whispered.

Danny followed him down the hall, and they stopped in a doorway. Danny stopped dead still. His heart stirred violently. He had always imagined he would see his child in Evey's arms, but he had thought this would never happen after their ugly split and to see it now made his heart leap in his chest.

Anthony walked around Danny and went to Evey and bent down and kissed her.

"Oh, babe, you are dirty! Go shower and then come love on me!" she shrieked in a quiet tone.

Anthony chuckled and said, "Fine."

"Danny, your room is right this way. You can set your bag down and then go see Ana," Anthony told him.

Danny followed him to a nice room with a desk and a futon bed. Anthony pointed to the bathroom along the way. Danny sat his bag down and took a deep breath. He needed to steady himself before he looked at his child in Evey's arms.

He walked across the hall back to the baby's room. Evey was still rocking Ana. Danny walked over to her and bent to his knees in front of her. He wanted so badly to put his arms around Evey's waist and pull them both close, but he didn't. Instead, he took his hand and gently rubbed a finger across Ana's cheek.

"She does have my hair," he smiled. "Funny. I wonder if there's ever been a blonde Indian."

"So far, she has blue eyes too. I don't think they're going to change," Evey said, putting her hand on Danny's shoulder.

He looked up at her with tears in his eyes.

"I'm so sorry, Evey. You shouldn't have to be going through all of this. You are still caught in my messes and mistakes," he said, looking down.

"Danny, Ana is not a mistake. She is part of my best friend. She's the only thing left alive of her, and she's part of you. Her life is precious, and it matters, and I love her," Evey said, her eyes filled with tears now.

"God, Evey, I don't want to make you cry. I've done that enough," he said, his eyes filled with a deep sorrow.

She nodded at him. "How about you hold your daughter while I go finish dinner?"

His eyes went wide, and he said, "I've never held a baby before."

"There's nothing to it. Put your arms out and just remember to support her head," Evey told him.

He did as she said, and Evey placed Ana in the crook of his arms.

"She's so little," he breathed out, smiling.

He followed Evey to the kitchen. Danny smiled as she cut carrots and started rice. He felt like he was in an illusion. She was cooking him supper, and she was taking care of his child. This was his dream—only she didn't cook just for him. Her husband was in the shower, and the child wasn't hers; she was from his one-night stand. He felt like a despicable human being.

She turned around and looked at him, "See, you are doing just fine with her."

Anthony came out of the bathroom and froze as he saw Danny holding Ana. Ana was his daughter, not Danny's, as far as he was concerned. Danny turned to look at him and tried to smile. Ana woke up then and started to wail. Danny couldn't calm her, and Evey's hands were dirty. Anthony came down the hall to him and put his arms out toward Ana. Danny reluctantly gave his daughter to him.

Anthony held her to his chest and began to sing a song to her in a soft tenor in his language, and Ana immediately calmed. Danny's heart broke. He knew he couldn't take Ana home, but seeing her soothed by Anthony was a lot to handle. He saw the way Anthony looked at Ana, and he knew without a doubt that Anthony was her daddy. He may be her biological father, but Anthony was her daddy. He had been there for everything.

Anthony looked up to Danny and noticed the look in his eyes. And for the first time ever, Anthony's eyes softened toward him; and in that moment, Anthony understood that he was what Danny couldn't be.

Anthony walked into the kitchen, holding tiny Ana in his huge muscular arms.

He put one arm around Evey and kissed her cheek and said, "Mmm, smells good. Is Ana ready for a bottle?"

"She will be soon but probably needs a clean diaper more than anything," Evey replied, not looking up from the side she was preparing.

Danny watched them, and he couldn't help but feel jealous. They were a family. It was what he longed for, but it wasn't his. Anthony turned and walked out of the kitchen and down the hall to Ana's room.

"Danny, you can go with him and figure out how to change a diaper," Evey said, not turning around.

"I don't think so, Evey. I'm not her daddy. I wish I was, but it's clear to see who her daddy is," Danny told her with a deep sorrow in his chest.

Evey turned around and went and hugged Danny. Anthony heard the exchange, and he didn't mind too much that Evey went to comfort him. But hearing those words come out of his mouth made him ease a little.

They ate dinner while Evey fed Ana.

Anthony laughed and told her, "You're such a mommy feeding her with one hand and feeding yourself with the other."

Danny nodded in agreement.

"I'm quite taken with this little one. I had no idea I was missing anything in my life until I held this little girl," Evey said, smiling down at the feeding baby.

Danny's heart was warm knowing that the woman he loved, loved his daughter.

After dinner, they moved to the living room.

"I hate to even ask, but I have to" Danny said. "What's happening with the investigation?"

"Nothing. Absolutely nothing. They couldn't find the bullet, and doing stuff on Indian land is very tricky, so they are just shelving it," Anthony answered in disgust.

Danny flushed in anger.

"That's just ridiculous. Is there anything I can do to help? I could hire a private investigator," Danny offered.

"That's nice, Danny, but we will figure it out," Evey said.

"Okay, one more question. Do you still have the check from my mother?" Danny asked.

"Yes. I do. Lola let me know where it was. I have it in the top drawer of Ana's dresser. Do you want it?" Evey asked.

"No. I want you to go deposit it and use it for Ana, and when that runs out, I want to know. I will help with anything. I know I can't raise her, and she is loved and secure here. I would never rip her from the only family she knows. Plus, I couldn't take her home to my mother. That wouldn't be fair to her, and I have no clue how to raise a child, much less do it on my own.

"I'm not going to lie, this hurts like hell. I see my eyes and hair and just want to hold her close and protect her, but the only way I can protect her is by not bringing her into my messed-up situation. I love her though. Will you please let her know of me and let her know I love her so much that I left her to have a happy life? She is my firstborn, so I will have her get a substantial portion of my Bailey inheritance when I go.

"And if it's okay with you, I'd like to leave something to any children you have. They will be Ana's siblings, and I know I will love any of your children, Evey. I'm sorry for striking a nerve, Anthony. I know that's probably the last thing you want to hear. But I'd like to do for all of your kids as I do for Ana," Danny explained.

Anthony did stiffen. His face went carefully blank.

"Danny, that's more than generous," Anthony said. "We cannot possibly accept that. You will have children of your own one day. And we will of course let Ana know of your love and sacrifice for her. You are a strong man for letting her go. I can't imagine what you are feeling. I love her as if she is my own flesh and blood and will always treat her as such."

Danny nodded and said, "All the same. I would like to give to all the children. Hell, maybe I can be crazy Uncle Danny. I think I could be a good uncle."

"Danny, we haven't filled out her birth certificate yet. We were waiting to decide on her full name," Evey looked at Anthony and squeezed his hand. "How do you feel about Ana Danielle Contararo? I'd like to pay some sort of tribute to you for your selflessness for your daughter. She could have a part of you in name at least."

Danny had tears fill his eyes, and he said, "I would be honored and proud."

The weekend went uneventfully. Danny took in as much of Ana as he could while he was there. He left a golden locket for her. It had a picture of him in it and a *B* engraved on the front. Danny did look at the check in the top drawer, and his stomach turned over. He couldn't imagine a world without Ana in it, even if he wasn't going to be the one raising her. Danny thought how life was an uphill battle to him. The woman whom he loved would raise his child with a man who was better than he. He supposed he deserved it. His child's mother was murdered, and his mother tried to have her aborted. Life just sucked.

Leaving was going to be hard, but he did it. He didn't shed a tear until he got back on the bus. He wasn't sure how he would just go on with life as if nothing happened when he got home. He had seen Ana and loved her deeply. Evey had even wished him happiness. How could she? He had singlehandedly turned her life upside down twice now. The only thing that had him at ease was knowing his daughter was in the best possible hands. He was even okay with Anthony being her daddy. He had to admit he was good with her and loved her.

Chapter 36

Anthony, Evey, Ana, and Tudley all sat on the front porch watching the sun go down. Anthony and Evey were reflecting over their weekend. It had gone surprisingly well with Danny, and they all felt some closure. But there was no closure where Lola was concerned.

Anthony's brows were bunched together as he thought about her murder and seeing Evey holding Lola on the pathway. His people would not rest easy knowing that her murderer was still out there, and this happening so soon in his reign as chief was already a dark blot.

"You're thinking of the investigation, aren't you?" Evey asked him, studying him.

He nodded and said, "I just can't get over them finding nothing. It's as if it were a personal hit. Whoever it was knew that she would be coming to find you and Analac. I don't know. Maybe I can find something else."

He let out a ragged breath.

Evey hated to see her husband so upset, but the truth was, she was too. Her best friend was gone, and little Ana lost her mother before she even got to set eyes on her.

Evey let her head fall on Anthony's shoulder, and she turned and kissed it. Then she overhead a redhead woodpecker flew over and starting to hammer out a beat on a tree. Evey looked over at it and studied it. She felt Analac was present when the woodpecker showed up.

"Analac visits on the wings of that woodpecker," Evey said to Anthony, pointing her chin toward it.

"She would be a woodpecker with the way she loved her trees," Anthony said, smiling.

A lightbulb went off in Evey's head. Analac's words rang in her head, "*My gift I pass to you. You call on the trees for good, and you call on my spirit when you need me.*"

"Anthony, I can find out who did it," she whispered.

He looked at her with question in his eyes.

"Analac told me. She gave me her gift. She told me to call on the trees for good and to use my gift wisely. I'm terrified to see who it was, but I won't let you have a dark blot on your record so soon, and I won't let my friend rest without finding justice for her and our daughter. Do you think you can help me find the section of trees someone would probably have stood in when they . . . they . . ." Evey trailed off, and Anthony wrapped her in his arms tight. She didn't need to finish her sentence.

He just said, "I think so."

Anthony held Evey in his arms tight all night. She felt cold and was uneasy. She knew what she would have to do, but she wasn't sure how it would work or if they would find the right spot. She prayed that she wouldn't have to see the act happen. She wasn't sure if the trees just spoke or if when she placed her hands on it, she would see. She was terrified, and she shivered even though it wasn't cold. Anthony lay awake holding her. He was upset that his wife had to do this. Evey was gifted, and she would use those gifts, whether he was okay with it or not. One thing was for sure—she wouldn't be alone.

Belle came over the next morning. Evey had called her and asked her if she could watch Ana for a couple hours. She was excited to, and she came right over. When she got there, she was surprised to see Anthony still there. Evey told her what they were about to do, and Belle nodded her approval.

"This is going to be very difficult on you, daughter. You are strong though. Don't be discouraged if it takes a few tries. This will be your first time to talk to the trees. I will whisper to the wind to help guide you too. I love you," Belle said, hugging her.

"I love you too," Evey said.

Anthony had his backpack filled with water and snacks and a knife. They went out to walk the path toward the woods. Evey's legs trembled, and she held onto Anthony's arm for stability.

They walked to the spot where Evey had held Lola the moments after she was shot.

Evey let out a loud scream as she bent to the bloodstained earth. She cried and let her tears mix with red-stained dirt to make mud, and then she spotted Lola's bracelet. With all the baby excitement and Analac's decision to take the baby's place, they had forgotten to get it. Evey picked it up carefully, to not get it in her palm and held it to her chest. She put it in Anthony's backpack. She would hold on to it for Ana.

"Okay, Evey. Here's the hard part. You and Analac were walking down from this way," Anthony said, motioning a little ways up. "And then Lola was coming from this way."

He pointed up the road.

"Where were you when you heard the bullet go by?" He asked her.

Evey stiffened, trying to regain her composure. She got up and walked back a good ways.

"I was here when I heard it and saw Lola crumble," she said.

Anthony walked toward her and looked back toward the woods. He was surveying them as if he were hunting—where he would hide to take a shot and where the best cover was.

He looked for a long while and then spotted a tree with a forked trunk.

If I were using a long rifle, that tree would be a good base for the barrel, and I could hide behind either trunk, Anthony deduced. *And in the chaos that follows, sneaking off through the back of the woods would be easy to do without being noticed.*

"This way," Anthony said, taking Evey's hand, as he led her toward the forked tree.

At the edge of the trees, Evey took a deep breath and began to sing the song that Analac had taught her:

Tales in trees, come talk to me. I promise to speak truth.
Tales in trees, come set your spirit free in me.
Tales in trees, in ancient way your secret will stay.
Tales in trees, I come to thee with a listening heart true.
Tales in trees, let me see what you'd have me do.
Tales in trees, come talk to me.

She listened but didn't hear anything. She felt numb. She kept singing it over and over but nothing. She let out a sigh.

In their tongue, she said, "Analac, speaker to the trees, send your spirit to guide me. Make sure my heart is right and true and show me the way."

Anthony stared at her and acted like this was just an everyday thing. Evey stood with her eyes closed, palms raised to the sky, listening. She heard something.

"*This way, granddaughter,*" a voice so familiar to her whispered.

She opened her eyes, still looking up, and she saw the redhead woodpecker fly overhead. She followed its path. It landed not on the forked tree but two trees behind it.

Evey sang the song again with confidence as she walked around the tree, and as she said the last word, she placed her hands on the tree. She heard dull whispers, and then, it was more like a roar in her ears.

She whispered to the tree, not knowing if what she did was right, "Can you help me? My friend lost her life, and we seek justice. Please. Can you tell me?"

Now she heard a soft chant in her head. Then she understood— it was the most beautiful voice, a voice of great wisdom.

"*Child, you may not like what you hear. Once you know, you have to use the knowledge wisely. You were a chosen one, so we will have faith our great sister chose wisely.*"

"I will choose wisely, and if it's okay, I would like to seek your wisdom," Evey spoke back in her head. "I'm smart enough to know I hold not all the answers. I shall ask again, can you tell me who shot my sister?"

"*So be it,*" the voice came back. "*The one you seek lives in your village. They are closer than you to your sister. She was ashamed and held a grudge. Jealously can turn the most beautiful person into the ugliest of souls. She prowls on the edge of town as the sun goes down. You will find her where the water wells, so my family tells me."*

Evey lay her head on the tree.

"Thank you, wise one. Thank you. Thank you for your kindness to me. What would you have me do?" she asked.

"Wise one, you are. Remember to ask. Seek what is right. Justice shall be served, and it will be served by your husband's hand. He will lead his people well," the wise voice said unto her.

Evey found herself kissing the tree. It was odd but felt right.

"Thank you, wise one. I shall come back and sit at your roots to reflect with you on the morrow," Evey replied silently.

"Go then, my child, and find your justice," the tree said, and the conversation was over as quickly as it started.

Evey opened her eyes and backed away from the tree, and she gave the woodpecker a silent thank-you. Anthony was staring at her.

"This wise one said the one I seek lives here and was closer to my sister than I. The wise one also said that she prowls on the edge of town as the sun goes down where the water wells. Do you know where that is?" Evey asked.

Anthony's eyes went wide.

"There is a natural spring that fills up a shallow pool. The water is said to well there, and it kept our people alive for many, many years. I can take you there. It's considered a sacred spot," he explained to her.

They went back to check on Belle and Ana. They were doing just fine. Belle was eating up all the baby cuddles. Evey and Anthony told Belle what they had found out.

She continued to rock as she asked, "Anthony, as chief, what do you plan to do now?"

Anthony thought for a moment.

"I am going to call the lead investigator and tell him that I heard word around town that our murderer will be in the sacred spot and that my wife and I intend on interrogating the suspect and would like them to sit back and be present. As soon as we hear a confession, they come in and take over," he said, rubbing his chin.

Belle nodded and said, "Hopefully they won't be armed. Remember, this person just shot Lola in cold blood. But I respect your choice, and I think handling within our tribe first is a good example to start."

Evey shuddered. She was nervous and sick to see who it would be. Lola wasn't exactly a friend to any of the young girls, and she almost wondered if Mrs. Bailey snuck up to take care of it. But that wasn't possible, seeing how whoever it was lived in the village.

Anthony called the investigator and explained the situation. They agreed to do it Anthony's way, and four officers came over to their house to discuss the particulars. Anthony and Evey would walk out seemingly alone, and the investigators would lurk back, wiring Anthony so everything would be heard and recorded.

They waited until it was close to sundown and headed toward the pool.

Evey's heart was in her throat. She wasn't sure how she would react to being in front of Lola's killer. This person had singlehandedly created the worst day of Evey's life, besides losing her parents.

They continued on in silence. Evey cried out in her head to the spirits of her ancestors. Anthony put his arm around her to steady her. They would do this together. They approached the pool and heard voices, a man and a woman. As they got closer, their forms started to take shape in the dimming light. Evey would have thought this place was beautiful, had it not been for why they were going.

She came to a lurch when her eyes met Lola's mother's. A flash of recognition shot through both women. Lola's father was there too, and he was building a small fire.

"Why are you building a fire on sacred ground brother?" Anthony asked.

The man looked in horror.

"Chief, I, um, I was just trying to set the soul of my daughter free," he responded.

Evey never let her eyes leave Lola's mother.

"Her soul is not yours to set free," Evey said firmly.

"She was my daughter, and I, uh . . . well, this is what I thought I could do for her," he said, shaking.

Then in the quiet distance, Evey heard the wise voice in her heard, *"Daughter, they light that fire that your sister's spirit may not haunt them."*

Both of Lola's parents looked at Evey, startled. Evey had her head titled sideways listening to something.

Evey looked up straight at them and asked, "Why are you worried about Lola's spirit haunting you?"

They both shifted uncomfortably. Anthony squeezed his arm around her to calm her.

"I asked a question. Why are you worried?" Evey asked again.

"We did disown her and threw her out, and the baby . . . I guess she has a reason to do so," her father said.

Evey looked to her mother. "And you? What's your reason?"

"I follow my husband's instruction," she said.

Anthony laughed at this. "I've known you my whole life and know that not to be true."

"What happens behind closed doors, you know nothing about," Lola's mother snapped at Anthony.

"But I know," said Evey. "I know you beat your daughter. I know you were jealous of her, and I know you despised her for finding a real family. Is that why you killed her?"

Lola's mother went pale.

"I did no such thing," she stuttered.

"Oh, so was it you then?" Evey said, looking at Lola's father.

He shook his head no and said, "I may have been upset with her choices and her being pregnant, but I would never hurt her."

Evey looked back at her mother now.

"Tell me the truth. I deserve the truth. I held Lola as she bled and gasped for breath. I held her as she struggled with pain as she breathed. I held her as she told me to take care of her baby. I held her as she let me see everything. I know exactly who you are and how you were to her. Tell me the truth," Evey demanded.

Lola's mother let an ugly smirk cross her lips.

"I did kill her. When I saw her head up the path toward the trees, I knew she would be alone on her way to find Analac. I didn't know you would be there or she and her bastard would both be gone. It was so easy. I just grabbed the rifle and shot, and while you were slumped over her, I just shrank back in the shadows. When I saw that bastard with blonde hair and blue eyes, I was disgusted. I held out hope that just maybe it was Anthony's and our people would live on. But to see one of your kind in that child. I couldn't bear it.

"But of course, you and Anthony will save the day and raise it. Lola didn't deserve recognition for being a whore. She didn't deserve to be placed at the high table. I had tried so hard for years to be there. And then she gets pregnant with a bastard child that is not of our people, and she's welcomed right in. You all disgust me."

Anthony broke in now.

"You don't insult my wife or my daughter. My wife is one of us, and so is my daughter. You are not one of us, and from this day forward, your name will mean nothing among our people, and you will forever be banned from stepping foot on our land."

"Aren't you the saving grace. You are a dumb young boy who will never be a true leader," Lola's mother said.

Anthony looked at Evey. He was concerned. He had never seen his wife so upset and filled with rage. She had her fists clenched and was shaking. She looked like she could erupt like a volcano, and Lola's mother's awful comments were just adding fuel to the fire.

Lola's father broke in now.

"You killed her? How could you? With my gun?"

She didn't answer him. She kept her eyes on Evey.

"Our people are known for their goodness and kindness and willingness to care for those in need. You are no such person," Evey spoke in their tongue.

The wind was blowing around them and making leaves swirl. Evey felt herself glaring at the woman.

"What is wrong with your eyes?" Lola's mother said, breath coming out of her.

Evey had no clue what she was talking about. She knew she could feel a fire burning her from the inside out, and she was angry. Her clinched fists at her sides felt like they were on fire. She glanced at her eyes in the pool for a split second and saw that they were burning a bright gold. She knew those eyes. They were the eyes she saw on her ancestor as she was burned alive in her bed. But her eyes burned from the fire consuming her. This fire was inside Evey.

In a quick motion, Lola's mother was lunging at Evey across the small fire that Lola's father had built, holding with a small herb knife in hand. Evey had no time to react, and Anthony leaped to get in front of his wife.

The fire inside Evey welled up, and she couldn't control it. A primal instinct kicked in, and it was not only that the fire was inside Evey—something else was too. And a knowing tingle hit Evey at her core. Evey raised her clenched hands up in a faster motion than Lola's leaping mother and released her fingers toward the sky.

The small fire Lola's father built went up in a huge roar. Before Lola's mother could reach her or Anthony, the flames took her. The piercing scream was more than Evey could bear. The police rushed in to clear the scene and to pull the woman from the flames. The nightmare was hopefully over.

As exhaustion took over Evey, she fell into Anthony. He caught her in a swift outward throw of his arms.

As she fell into unconsciousness into Anthony's arms, in their tongue, she said, "Not only is the fire within me, so is your child."